Dear Reader,

W9-DDR-933

What could be more romantic than a wedding? Picture the bride in an exquisite gown, with flowers cascading from the glorious bouquet in her hand. Imagine the handsome groom in a finely tailored tuxedo, his eyes sparkling with happiness and love. Hear them promise "to have and to hold" each other forever. . . . This is the perfect ending to a courtship, the blessed ritual we cherish in our hearts. And now, in honor of the tradition of June brides, we present a month's line-up of six LOVESWEPTs with beautiful brides and gorgeous grooms on the covers.

Don't miss any of our brides and grooms this month:

There's no better way to celebrate the joy of weddings than with all six LOVESWEPTs, each one a fabulous love story written by only the best in the genre!

With best wishes,

Nita Taublib
Associate Publisher/LOVESWEPT

WHAT ARE *LOVESWEPT* ROMANCES?

They are stories of true romance and touching emotion. We believe those two very important ingredients are constants in our highly sensual and very believable stories in the *LOVESWEPT* line. Our goal is to give you, the reader, stories of consistently high quality that may sometimes make you laugh, sometimes make you cry, but are always fresh and creative and contain many delightful surprises within their pages.

Most romance fans read an enormous number of books. Those they truly love, they keep. Others may be traded with friends and soon forgotten. We hope that each *LOVESWEPT* romance will be a treasure—a "keeper." We will always try to publish

LOVE STORIES YOU'LL NEVER FORGET
BY AUTHORS YOU'LL ALWAYS REMEMBER

The Editors

Victoria Leigh
Where There's a Will . . .

BANTAM BOOKS
NEW YORK · TORONTO · LONDON · SYDNEY · AUCKLAND

WHERE THERE'S A WILL . . .

A Bantam Book / July 1992

If you would be interested in receiving protective vinyl
covers for your Loveswept books, please write to this address
for information:

Loveswept
Bantam Books
P.O. Box 985
Hicksville, NY 11802

ISBN 0-553-44231-7

Published simultaneously in the United States and Canada

PRINTED IN THE UNITED STATES OF AMERICA

OPM   0 9 8 7 6 5 4 3 2 1

Prologue

"Beginner, intermediate, or advanced?"

"Excuse me?"

The young man smiled at the diminutive blonde on the customer side of the ski rentals counter and repeated himself. "Are you a beginner, intermediate, or advanced skier?"

"What does that have to do with what kind of skis I want to rent?" she asked, bewilderment clearly apparent in her voice.

"I'm just trying to get a feel for what equipment will do the best job for you," Scott answered with the infinite patience of one who was at the beginning of his work shift.

"Oh, I already know what I need." The woman gave Scott a sunny smile and pointed toward a pair of skis propped against the end of a rack of skis that hung in rows behind the desk. "Those turquoise ones with the pretty pink birds will do nicely."

Casually, Will Jackson moved closer until he was just a few feet behind the female half of the conversation. Pretending to examine a pair of goggles, he studied her in the mirror that angled down from the ceiling and ran the length of the shop. She was rather pretty, he thought, blond and fair and not so young as to make him feel like a lecher. Her almost total lack of makeup showed off an exquisite milk-and-honey complexion that was usually reserved for classic English beauties. Her eyes were gray-green, her lashes long. Lips the color of a desert rose were slightly parted as she smiled up at Scott.

Not a head turner, Will decided, but still quite nice to look at. Her appearance, though, wasn't what had caught his attention as he waited for his chance to corner Scott about the Old Geezers' Slalom Race the following weekend. While Scott was not old enough to qualify for a spot on any of the teams, Will was planning on extracting a hefty prize from the shop that Scott managed for his father.

Will edged closer to the pair, not wanting to miss a single word of their conversation. That soft, husky voice of hers was exquisitely exciting, and their dialogue was the most entertainment he'd had in weeks. Will knew that "those turquoise ones with the pretty pink birds" were Scott's brand-new, custom-designed, hand-painted skis. He'd probably brought them into the shop for waxing. Or just to pet in his spare time.

Either way, those skis were definitely not for rent.

"Those skis aren't for rent," Scott said with an indulgent grin.

"My outfit is turquoise with splashes of coral," the blonde said earnestly, without any notice of Scott's statement. "Coral, not pink like the birds. I hope that won't be a problem," she added almost to herself as Scott edged defensively between the woman and his prized possessions.

"Those are *my* skis," he said, a touch of nervousness shading his assertion.

"Nonsense! They're sitting right under that Rentals sign."

Scott glanced up at the sign and then back at the woman, who was showing no evidence of paying him any mind whatsoever. Her brows were knit in momentary annoyance and she craned her neck in an attempt to see around him. Thwarted by his deliberately obstructive posture, she quickly scooted around the counter and was studying the skis at close range before Scott could intervene.

He cleared his throat and tried another tack. "As a general rule, we like to match the equipment with skill level. It makes for less chaos on the slopes that way."

The blonde laughed as though Scott was being particularly amusing, then apparently decided to humor him when he didn't even crack a smile. "What level are these?" she asked, stroking one brilliantly painted ski with a proprietary air.

"They're fast," Scott said in a panicked rush. "I wouldn't recommend them for anyone who is less than an advanced-intermediate skier."

"*I'm* an advanced-intermediate skier," she pronounced, fibbing with a transparency that wouldn't have fooled a child.

Will watched as Scott verged on calling her a liar. He didn't, though, and Will gave him marks for diplomacy, which more than made up for his tactical error of talking about renting his precious skis at all.

Switching his gaze back to the woman's reflection, Will studied her delicate features again.

She didn't look at all loony, he mused, and wondered what it was about her that hinted at a rational mind she'd thus far managed not to exhibit. With an unexpected touch of disappointment, he had to admit that the blonde was as daft as she was pretty. Anyone who would risk her life on equipment she wasn't capable of controlling had more than one screw loose.

Still, he waited for her to speak again. Her voice—so husky, so sexily feminine—was addictive. There was something behind her words too. Laughter, he was inclined to believe, yet knew he must be mistaken. The blonde was completely serious. Holding a coral-tipped finger alongside a pink flamingo she considered the colors, a speculative gleam in her eyes.

"Coral and pink aren't so bad," she murmured just

loudly enough for Will to hear. "This turquoise, though. What if it clashes with my jacket?"

All of the muscles in Scott's sun-bronzed face tightened with his determination not to react. Will watched for the explosion, fascinated and more than a little impressed when Scott's features settled into an impassive mask.

"Turquoise is *very* hard to match," he said with authority. "*I* certainly wouldn't take the chance."

"I *knew* I should have worn my jacket over here," she said as she nodded in agreement. "After all, I wouldn't dream of buying new shoes to match a dress without taking the dress along." She looked up at Scott apologetically and shrugged. "I guess renting skis is a lot like buying shoes. Who'd have thought?"

Will clenched his teeth against the chuckle that threatened to expose his eavesdropping. Scott took similar measures to contain his own mirth. Now that his personal property was no longer in imminent danger of premature destruction, the younger man appeared to relax.

"What if I found you a pair of pink ones?" he asked slyly.

"Coral," she said.

"Coral goes with pink much better than two different shades of turquoise," he said, as though he knew what he was talking about.

"You're sure?"

"Absolutely."

She appeared to think about it for a long moment before finally nodding in agreement to this piece of wisdom.

Scott didn't give her a chance to change her mind. Plucking a pair of bright-pink skis from the overhead rack—Will looked at the make and knew they were short and flexible enough for an absolute beginner—Scott leaned them against the counter and said, "Now we need to fit you for boots."

"I think those white ones with the gold lightning on the sides will do me fine," she said. Will was positive he detected a groan from Scott as he followed the direction of her gaze.

Top-of-the-line boots. Only the most experienced skiers had even heard of them. Definitely overkill for a beginner—not to mention the chance they'd come back scarred and battered. Will laughed aloud this time, totally uncaring when the blonde turned to stare curiously at him. She looked back at Scott. "Are those for rent?"

Scott gulped and nodded, then brightened as he apparently found a way out. "What size do you wear?" he asked.

Check. Will smiled, admiring Scott's quick thinking.

The blonde took his measure with a narrowed gaze. "What size do they come in?" she asked softly.

Checkmate. Will couldn't take any more. He strolled to the far end of the shop and considered the likelihood that the blonde wasn't as dumb as she acted.

He was staring out the thick-paned window when she finally left the shop, the white boots with gold lightning on the sides clasped trophylike in her arms. A feeling akin to pride filled him, and his gaze tracked her progress across the tiny parking lot to a bright-orange Volkswagen Beetle. Scott trailed behind her with the skis and poles, and together they stuffed the equipment into the car.

Will watched until the little orange car roared out of the parking lot, its chained tires clutching at the icy street as it sped away.

It bothered him that he didn't even know her name.

One

Maggie Cooper propped her hips against the bathroom counter and concentrated on what she was doing. Stroking the tiny cosmetic brush across one eyelid, she tried to gauge the narrow margin between subtle and sexy. It would make a difference.

Subtlety wouldn't net her a thing.

Cautiously, she added another stroke of eye shadow and hummed under her breath. She'd been humming off and on for an hour now, ever since the hotel's disco, one floor below her room, had cranked up the amps. Maggie was grateful for the distraction.

She could feel the music right through the floor. The heavy bass sent up a rhythmic thrumming that tickled the nerve endings of her bare feet. It was a good thing she didn't mind being rocked to sleep, she mused, throwing a dry towel onto the tiled floor of the bathroom and stepping on it. Her feet were cold and the tiles weren't helping.

Cold feet. That pretty much said it all. The rising pitch of the band reminded her that Lake Tahoe's nightlife was in full swing. If she didn't get her act together she'd still be in her room at midnight—alone—and that wouldn't do at all.

She leaned closer to the mirror, her hand shaking a little. She'd already had to wash the eye shadow off three times, and if she didn't get it right she'd look like a clown. If she hadn't been sure that the type of woman she was determined to emulate that night would wear more makeup than she normally applied, she wouldn't be bothering with it.

But if she didn't get downstairs soon, the night would be wasted and she'd have to spend another interminable day wondering what it would be like to seduce a stranger.

Darn it! She'd botched it again!

Cursing with limited fluency, Maggie shifted her hips. They were rubbing against the counter, and she had to stand on her toes to alleviate the pressure. "I'll bet normal-size people don't even know what toes are for," she muttered, her calves straining as she used every bit of added elevation to get closer to the mirror.

Not that she minded being small; *petite* as some called it. She was five feet three inches tall, although her doctor said it was more like five feet one, because it didn't count if you stood on your toes. Maggie didn't pay him any mind. A person was as tall as she felt, and she felt about five feet three inches. To underscore the point that height was not a problem with her she usually wore flats, saving higher heels for special occasions.

Leaning into the mirror, she gritted her teeth and gave it one more try. With a determined hand, she spread the shell-pink powder across both lids. She gave the mauve-coated sponge applicator a threatening scowl, then stroked the shadow on in the prescribed manner—quickly, because if it didn't work this time she was going to wash it all off and get on with the rest of her life. It worked, though, maybe because she no longer cared, and Maggie grinned at her reflection for a moment before grabbing the tube of mascara.

This part was easy. She'd had lots of practice applying the light brown accent to her white-blond lashes. A couple flips of her wrist and she had eyelashes, their luxurious length and thickness now visible. They called her "Mole Eyes" at the office, never failing to razz her on those days when she was too lazy or too late to bother with mascara. Without it, her eyes were all iris and pupils without a complementing frame, large gray-green orbs staring out from a pale, undefined background.

She didn't have to wonder what her coworkers would think of her now. Vacaville, California, was certainly not an unsophisticated town, considering that San Francisco was near enough for dinner or the theater. She'd led a quiet life since moving to Vacaville several years earlier, though, keeping to herself and giving the impression that she was shy. Reserved. Perhaps even a little aloof.

They'd never recognize the Maggie that was reflected in the mirror—a woman intent upon seduction.

She whipped the rosy blush across her cheeks, then threw the brush onto the counter. Out of habit, she straightened the mess she'd made, pushing the cosmetics into a drawer and grabbing the new tube of deep red lipstick before it fell inside with the rest. She smoothed it across her lips, then tried not to look at the finished product. It was only her face and what was the big deal if she looked like a hooker?

Hooker! Frantically she examined her reflection, because that was not the image she was seeking. She exhaled a relieved sigh when she found she'd not really gone overboard, just a little more eye shadow than she was accustomed to. That was all, nothing to get excited about. And her lips were full and soft. Voluptuous, even.

Did she look sexy? She hoped so. But could she act sexy?

It was certainly a challenge. She pursed her lips, wondering if she'd bitten off more than she could chew with the sexy role she was about to play.

The airhead half of her new persona—Bambi Bubblehead by name—had made its trial run at the ski rentals place earlier that afternoon with stupefying results.

She'd left there knowing the clerk believed her totally devoid of a single rational thought.

The other man who'd overheard the ditzy dialogue had seemed likewise impressed. Maggie grinned. It was fun playing the part of a bubblehead. And necessary. She wasn't convinced she could play the seductress with a straight face for any length of time. A ditzy seductress, however, could be excused for hashing up a sizzling scene or for giggling at inopportune moments.

She rechecked the physical side of the alter ego she'd created, noticing for the first time that she'd forgotten to brush her hair. The short blond waves were sticking out in a few places where she'd dragged her fingers through them during the trial of adding color and excitement to her eyes. Picking up the brush, she attempted to order it into the natural style she preferred, a few wisps curling here and there and then tapering to a smooth line at her nape. As always, it took on a life of its own, self-styling, really, because it was thick and very, very fine.

It was close to nine by the time she made herself quit stalling and put down the brush. But she'd forgotten the perfume and was grateful for the few seconds it took to uncap the bottle of a quarter ounce of the most expensive scent she'd ever worn. She dabbed it on her wrists, stroked a little behind her ears, then wondered if she should put some on the back of her knees. The redheaded bombshell in the movie she'd watched the night before had done that, but Maggie didn't have the gall. Besides, who was going to sniff her knees?

That was what this night was all about, though, she reminded herself, sniffing knees or whatever. With deliberate care, she reached down and applied the perfume, then straightened before the blood rushed to her face. Her fingers shook as she screwed the cap tightly back on the perfume bottle.

She walked into the bedroom, and the creamy silk and lace camisole she wore shimmied against her skin. The sensual caress reminded her—just in case she'd managed to forget—that she had certain goals to accomplish that night, and if she didn't get moving everyone would be asleep and she'd have wasted all this effort for nothing.

Working quickly now, ignoring hands that were still unsteady, she pulled on the soft wool slacks she'd left draped across one of the two easy chairs that occupied a corner of the large room. Next, she grabbed the matching ice-pink cashmere sweater and pulled it over her head. Of course, that meant she had to brush her hair again. She didn't waste more than a moment, hurrying back to the bathroom and dragging the brush through her hair.

She stared at her reflection and wondered who was looking back at her, because the woman in the mirror certainly wasn't anyone she knew.

It was the eyes, she decided. Not the unaccustomed eye shadow, but their expression—determined and scared and excited all at once. She was committed now.

She swept back into the bedroom, tidying everything, making sure the cognac was on the tray with the cut-crystal snifters she'd brought from home. She wondered if he'd even notice the special touches, not that it mattered. She wasn't bringing him up to her room for any reason other than to find out something about herself.

Impatient now, she tugged a wrinkle from the bedspread and slipped into her shoes. The soft off-white leather flats were comfortable from a hundred wearings, reassuring in a friendly sort of way.

Her journal lay at the corner of the bed, the brown calfskin cover scarred by the years of laughter, tears, and everyday living she'd recorded therein. She started toward it, tempted to take a minute to jot down a few lines. Self-knowledge stopped her in her tracks. It was so easy for Maggie to lose herself in her writing, and a few minutes could easily turn into an hour or more.

She bypassed the journal and went to the door, promising herself that there would be plenty of time tomorrow to record her tumultuous emotions . . . and whatever adventures she encountered this night. The lapse of a few hours might put a better perspective on everything, she told herself.

Up to the very last moment she knew she still had a choice. She could leave her room and make her way to the lounge, which was at the opposite end of the building, far away from the throbbing beat of the disco, and find someone there who was attracted by the image she presented, a man who would give her the answers she needed so badly.

Or she could stay in her room, alone, and never know for sure if Charles, her ex-husband, had been right. *You're sexless and inhibited and cold.* The words still felt as harsh as the first time he'd said them, the pain they'd caused unmitigated by the years since their divorce.

She knew he must be wrong. He *had* to be. She opened the door with a hand that was suddenly steady. She'd come to this anonymous hotel to prove her sexuality, her desirability. She hoped there was an adequate number of suitable victims below. She had just three nights to find a man who could make her feel like a woman.

Striding down the carpeted hallway she rehearsed her lines, taking as much care with those as she had with her appearance. Acting the part of a bubble-head wasn't as easy as it looked.

Will half listened as Casey spoke quietly with the reception manager. Without removing his attention from the woman he'd been watching for the last few minutes, he signaled Biff for another round.

She was still alone. Will took his gaze off her long enough to make sure the clown in the bright-red après-ski outfit hadn't moved any closer to her, because then he'd have to decide if he wanted to compete. He wasn't sure he was up for it, not even if it meant he'd have all night to listen to that sexy voice as they did . . . whatever it was she'd come there to do.

He wasn't interested, he told himself firmly.

It would probably be more fun to watch the two of them together, each of them such perfect stereotypes—the lounge lizard and the snow bunny. And while the entertainment would disappear the minute the lizard snaked her into leaving with him, it would be interesting to see how long it took.

His jaw clenched as he thought about the lizard putting his hands on her. It took several moments and a stern lecture to remind himself that it wasn't any of his business if the lizard managed to seduce her.

There were other unattached men in the room, of course, but they'd already made their approaches and been sent firmly away. That was why the lizard had waited, he supposed, biding his time until she wouldn't be so quick to reject his advances, for he'd be her only alternative left. He was certainly confident, Will thought as he watched the man preen without appearing to look at the woman. He worked his way slowly into her sphere of awareness, his gray-streaked hair at odds with the sun-bleached heads around him.

Clearly, he didn't consider Will competition. Maybe it was because he wasn't dressed like the others, set apart from the après-ski set by his light-brown corduroy jacket and darker wool slacks, his shirt a maroon pinstripe on white cotton. The tie was the most telling point that he probably wasn't there just for a weekend of spring skiing. There was also his familiarity with the staff, which probably helped the lizard decide he wasn't on the make.

So intent was he on the unfolding drama, Will didn't notice when his empty glass was replaced with a full one.

"I never would have pegged you for that type," Casey said as the reception manager got up and left the table.

"What type?" Lifting the soda water to his lips, Will gave the other man a deliberately slow look before letting his gaze return to the blonde. He'd not yet told his friend about the afternoon's entertainment at the rental shop. And he was fairly certain he wasn't going to.

"Ditzy blonde, of course," Casey said. "I thought you knew."

"She's blond," Will agreed, hiding a flash of irritation at Casey's assessment. Why he minded that assessment was a mystery to him. He'd made the same judgment himself only hours ago. Still, it didn't feel right having another man talk about her that way.

Even if it was true.

He shifted his lithe frame within the confines of the bar chair, leaning on the armrest as he continued studying her. She was as he remembered, although she'd been a little heavy-handed with the cosmetics tonight. Too bad, he thought. The woman beneath the artificial shadows and colors had been quite stunning earlier in the day. Not that she was an eyesore now. He just preferred her the other way, natural and fresh.

Will didn't even notice that he'd elevated her several levels up from "pretty."

At least she'd left her hair alone, he mused. He liked how she brushed it away from her face, the dark-blond waves highlighted by streaks of white gold. A nudge from Casey reminded him that his friend was waiting for the rest of his opinion on her.

"A bit overdone, I'll agree. But I'm afraid I don't see the ditzy part."

"She told Biff she was here for the skiing," Casey said, referring to the bartender, "and asked if it was proper to wear powder pants even though she didn't intend to go near the deep stuff unless she made a mistake and took the wrong lift. And then she confessed she'd only bought the powder pants because they were the right color and nothing else had even been close. She really didn't want to do any heavy skiing because then she'd be too worn out to have any fun at night."

Will thought about telling Casey that her outfit was turquoise with coral splashes. "What did Biff tell her?" he asked instead.

"That it would be their secret, and if she remembered to put some snow into her pockets before coming into the lodge, she could empty them in the lobby, pretend she'd been butt-deep in powder, and no one would be the wiser."

"Ditzy," Will murmured with a touch of regret as he continued to watch her from his corner table. She'd noticed him when he came in, had even turned her chair a little so she could look in his direction without turning her head more than a degree or two.

She remembered him, it seemed.

Her conspicuously flirtatious pursuit was surprisingly amusing. He'd almost laughed aloud when she'd pretended not to notice he'd noticed her—when he had finally allowed himself to gaze directly at her. It was all such a game, looking without seeming to look, as she was doing now. She lifted her gaze from her hands and stared across the room at him, meeting his eyes and acting as though she hadn't meant to do that. She colored for some reason he couldn't fathom, then dropped her lashes. He knew she was still watching him, though. He didn't look away, wanting to see what she'd do if he persisted.

After a long moment, she lifted her lashes just a fraction and dragged the pink tip of her tongue across her lips.

Arousal shot through his body without warning. He was suddenly hot with need. He wanted her. Tonight.

That wasn't like him at all. He preferred long-term affairs, not one-night stands. Relationships, not indiscriminate sex. And this woman was not even in the running for a relationship, he told himself sternly. Even if she wasn't as loony as she acted, there was still the distance problem. He'd heard her mention to Scott that she was from Vacaville, one of several towns that bordered the highway between Sacramento and San Francisco. It was also about a four hours' drive from the south shore of Lake Tahoe, where Will lived.

Long-distance relationships were simply more trouble than they were worth. Will congratulated himself on his impeccable logic as his body stirred with a longing that was extraordinarily emphatic.

He had absolutely no intention of giving in to this unexpected response.

She looked away, finally. Her color was higher, he thought, perhaps because he hadn't responded to her sensual invitation with anything more than a hot stare. He hadn't done what she'd wanted, which was to leave his table and join her, buy her a drink, take her to bed.

He breathed a sigh of relief that he hadn't succumbed. He liked to do his own hunting, although being on the other side of the game was a seductive experience.

"The lady is definitely trolling," Casey drawled.

Will flicked him a chiding glance. "You're not supposed to notice things like that. Harriet won't stand for it."

Casey laughed. "My wife realizes I'm not blind. Besides, I'm just showing an interest in *your* love life."

"Love?" Will snorted. He was old enough to know that the woman in pink was physically rather than emotionally motivated.

"Sex then?" Casey grinned as Will nodded his agreement. "Well, you have to admit she knows what she wants. In the hour since she walked in, she's weighed, measured, and cataloged every man in the room."

"So why is she still alone?"

"The ones she rejected probably didn't measure up to whatever scale she's using. And now I expect she's waiting for the Crimson Creeper to make his move. Unless you decide to ace him out, that is. But she can't tell if you're interested or not and she doesn't want to blow it with the other guy."

Crimson Creeper. Will laughed shortly and said, "She knows I'm interested. She just doesn't think I'm going to do anything about it."

"Are you?"

"I doubt it." A half-smile rested on his lips as he watched the woman direct her gaze toward the lizard. She was probably trying out the same come-hither lip trick she'd used on him. "I came to see you about that new advertising proposal you sent over." Shunting thoughts of the woman aside, he turned in his chair until Casey was his prime focus. "You knew I'd like their approach, didn't you?"

"It's different," Casey agreed, "but I didn't want to make any waves with the old agency until you'd checked it out." He went on to give Will a summary of his own impressions of the new ad agency. Will listened carefully, interrupting now and then with a question. He didn't have many.

As general manager of the hotel, Casey knew exactly what he was doing. As owner, Will was smart enough to let him do it. Will pretty much kept to the background, lending support when it was needed, staying out of the way when it wasn't. Major decisions such as this were usually handled without much fuss—they either agreed or they didn't. When they didn't, Will generally bowed to the other man's expertise and abdicated the decision to Casey.

Business hadn't been the only reason for his visit to the hotel that night. Short of disconnecting his phone and sitting in the dark, there was no way he could stay in his house. For the past month he'd been hounded day and night by a woman determined to marry him.

Will had no intention of complying.

When Cheryl had first raised the subject, he had gently but firmly reminded her that he'd warned her in the beginning. He wasn't interested in a permanent arrangement. With anyone. She'd smiled and suggested he might have changed his mind.

He hadn't. She persisted, he held his ground. She wouldn't take no for an answer. Apparently, no one had ever said no to the beautiful, exciting, *persistent* Cheryl.

When it became obvious she wouldn't be convinced, Will terminated their relationship altogether. She pursued him with renewed fervor.

He cursed Cheryl's tenacity under his breath. He really would prefer to be sitting in front of the fireplace in his den, reading or just listening to music, instead of calculating how long it would be before the woman in pink nailed her prey. It turned his stomach to think she'd end the night with the graying Romeo in designer rags—but it was none of his business.

The Crimson Creeper was finally making his move. Will hadn't missed the fact that the lizard had managed to get significantly closer to his goal, his back turned to the woman as he bent down to share a joke with the three-some occupying the adjacent booth. A slight turn of his head as he laughed, his shoulders rolling to present a side view of his supposedly handsome face, and the stage was set for his "noticing" the solitary occupant at the next table.

Will didn't care to watch the next scene.

He wrapped up the business of the evening by agreeing to whatever Casey wanted. Standing up, he was about to say good night and get out of there when a woman's voice interrupted.

"Will, darling," Cheryl said, her tone bright with just the right amount of happy surprise. "Imagine finding you here!"

He should have known she wouldn't be deterred when she didn't find him at home. He suffered the wet kiss she planted on his lips. Getting it over with was more expedient than trying to avoid the unavoidable. As soon as it was over, he backed up and calculated the distance to the exit.

"What do you want now, Cheryl?" he asked flatly. His gaze raked her skin-tight black catsuit with disinterest, then rose to meet eyes that were an unreal shade of emerald green, thanks to the contact lenses she wore. She was confident the outfit would sway him, he realized. He watched indifferently as she smoothed the slick fabric across one hip, her other hand lifting to tuck a heavy wave of ebony hair behind her ear.

She was trying to appear unruffled by his abrupt response. Smiling at Casey, she slipped into a chair and patted the one next to her in an invitation for Will to sit.

"Why don't the three of us have a drink, unless you have other things to do, Casey?" She looked as though she knew there were at least a dozen chores Casey needed to be doing.

Casey stayed where he was. Will shot him a grateful look as he examined his options. He could sit down and try to explain once again that he wasn't going to change his mind. Their affair was over and not even the sexy catsuit she wore would convince him otherwise.

He opted to stay on his feet. "Sorry, Cheryl, I have other plans."

She hadn't expected that. Frowning, she tried another angle. "If you're leaving, then would you mind giving me a ride? The ice on the roads is horrible. I'd feel better if I didn't have to drive home."

"I didn't say I was leaving. I said I have other plans. I'm sure Casey will find you a cab if you're really nervous." Reaching across the table, he picked up his unfinished drink, then turned his back on the two of them.

Will pulled out the chair beside the woman in pink just as the Crimson Creeper banked for his final approach.

Two

"Is your offer still open?"

He spoke softly, leaning down so she couldn't miss his words, and stroked his hand familiarly across her shoulder.

Maggie almost bit her tongue. His hand, so warm through the soft knit, and his voice sent shivers down her back. It was the shock of his touch, she decided, and was sorry when he dropped his hand. He'd taken her completely by surprise, coming over like that. She'd crossed him off her list of possible victims after he hadn't responded to her outrageous overture. He'd just sat there, staring. She could tell because of the tilt of his head, but she hadn't been able to read what was in his eyes. He'd been too far away. She'd imagined there was heat there, then dismissed that as wishful thinking. It was what she'd wanted to see.

The other man she'd considered, the one in the silly red jumpsuit who looked as though he'd played this game often, suddenly veered away. He was sucked back into the crowd of holiday makers, pretending he hadn't intended to approach her table at all. That was fine with Maggie. She hadn't liked the looks of him all that much, but had left herself open for his advances. She only had three nights and the choices might not get any better.

And now the pick of the litter was sliding into the chair beside her. His wavy dark-brown hair, blue-gray eyes, and tanned, rugged features looked even better than she remembered. He was tall and broad shouldered beneath the well-cut sport jacket, and she guessed there wasn't an ounce of fat anywhere on his body. He moved with an easy kind of grace that bespoke confidence in his physical condition. Her face just inches from his, she focused on the slight cleft in his chin.

It was adorable.

She was relieved. After her performance that afternoon, he was already well informed as to the bubble-head side of her personality. Obviously, he was still interested.

And she was annoyed. Maggie hated thinking she was actually attracted to a man who thought she was nothing more than a dumb blonde. She *was* attracted too. Only through uncommon willpower had she been able to ignore him in the shop that afternoon.

"What offer?" she squeaked, then cleared her throat and attempted to deepen her voice to a husky drawl. "What offer?" she asked again, forcing herself to meet his steady gaze.

"You know what I'm talking about," he said. "That little trick you do with your tongue is one hell of an invitation." His eyes narrowed as he considered an alternative. "Unless you're just a tease, of course."

"I'm not a tease," she said quickly when he looked as though he might get up and leave. The thought of starting all over with another man panicked her. "I guess I'm surprised, that's all." Her gaze trailed over his shoulder to the table he'd left and the gorgeous woman who was obviously fuming at his departure.

"You shouldn't be," Will murmured, leaning closer. He wanted Cheryl to see he wasn't just over there for a visit. It wasn't nice, using the woman like this, but she'd started it. He decided he could spend a couple of minutes finding out if he was interested. He wouldn't do anything about it, of course. Sex was an intimate experience between a man and a woman. He couldn't imagine doing it with a complete stranger.

It didn't stop him from wondering what it would be like, though.

"Do it again," he said, drawing her gaze away from Cheryl. Cheryl's kiss hadn't meant anything, and he didn't want her thinking about it.

"Do what again?"

"That thing with your tongue." He wanted to shock her—if she could be shocked. That was something else he wanted to find out. "It was arousing as hell and I want to see it close up."

Maggie gasped and ran her tongue across her suddenly dry lips. Then she realized she'd done exactly as he'd demanded. Her color deepened from pink to bright red. This won't do at all! she warned herself. She sucked in a deep breath as she searched for something in character to say, because that *idiotic blush* sure wasn't helping things!

"I like the blush too," he said. "It adds depth."

"Excuse me?"

"Women who flirt as blatantly as you generally can't do something so candid as blush. It's a contradiction that interests me."

"What else do you like?" she asked, swept along by the erotic flavor of their conversation. The sudden darkening of his eyes reassured her she'd said the right thing.

"I'm not sure yet," he said, "but I bet I'll find out before the night's over." That was nonsense, of course, Will told himself, but it was part of the game she was playing. It was what she expected to hear.

Maggie blushed again, and looked away for a moment in a futile attempt to hide it. She'd never imagined it would be like this, provocative words from a stranger that sent lightning bolts of excitement through her veins. She'd expected the words, but nothing could have prepared her for her response! Silently, she stared across the room as Biff, the bartender, flirted with a gorgeous pair of redheads and wondered what the man beside her would say next.

"Is this your first trip here?"

The totally unprovocative words rendered her speechless. She shook her head.

"Do you come to Tahoe often?"

"No." She thought she saw disappointment flicker in his eyes, but she must have been mistaken. Men looking for sexual flings wouldn't want the woman to stick around when it was over, would they? "I'm from Vacaville."

A shame, Will thought, as her words confirmed what he'd both known and guessed. A relationship was definitely out of the question if she rarely visited the lake.

Still, his interest had ripened from the first moment he'd heard her speak again. Her soft, husky voice played havoc with his heartbeat as her scent invaded his senses. She was a small woman, delicate . . . not at all his type, he reminded himself. He liked his women taller, stronger, a complement to his own size rather than a contrast.

Out of the corner of his eye, he saw Cheryl stalk out of the room. The smoke screen of another woman was no longer required. So why didn't he get up and leave?

He didn't want to. He decided to stick around for a while and find out why.

"May I buy you a drink?" he asked before he looked at the half-full glass of wine in front of her. He signaled the waiter anyway. There was something about this woman that made him thirsty.

"My mother told me never to accept drinks from strangers," Maggie said coyly, then cringed inside. She had sounded so prim and proper, and that was *not* the way she'd intended it.

"My name is Will Jackson," he said, and raised his eyebrows in the silent query.

"I'd like something cold and white," she said. She formed the words with deliberate care, knowing he was watching her lips. That was practically all he'd done since he'd sat down. After coming out with that line about cold and white, though, she found it amazingly difficult to keep a straight face. It had sounded so absurd! All she could do now was hope he didn't order a vodka on the rocks for her.

"I want to know your name," he said. He had to wait for it, though, because the waiter finally arrived. He ordered the drinks—white wine for her, soda water for him. "Your name?" he prompted when they were alone again.

All that rehearsal and she hadn't given any thought to a stage name! Maggie knew it was too late to come up with something sexy, so she kept her own moniker and did her best to flavor it with a sprinkle of ditz. "Margaret Ann Cooper—Mac to my friends, but you can call me Maggie. I've always wanted a nickname."

"Mac's not a nickname?" Will asked, and choked back his laughter when she appeared to think about it.

"No, it's an antonym. You know, M for Margaret, A for Ann, C for Cooper."

He decided not to tell her the word was *acronym*. It really didn't matter. He'd call her Maggie and let well enough alone.

"Do you plan to ski Heavenly Valley or one of the areas at the other end of the lake?" he asked.

"Heavenly, of course," she said. "I figured any area with a name like that would be skier friendly. If nothing else, the snow sounds softer."

"Softer?"

"For when I fall," she said with complete seriousness. "Heavenly reminds me of clouds and I figured the snow here might be softer. I should expect to fall, don't you think?"

A lot, from the sound of it, Will thought. In a confidential voice, he asked, "Maggie, do you really have any idea how to ski?"

She giggled once as though he'd asked a particularly silly question, then confessed that she'd lied to the man in the ski shop about her skill level. There had been only two holiday excursions with her school chums in Scotland, when her father had been stationed north of London with the air force. But Scotland had hills, not mountains like those outside, and she was pretty sure her skills were rusty.

"It's a good thing you took the pink skis instead of the others," he murmured. She knew less about the sport than he'd imagined, and it worried him.

She frowned. "You really think it would have made a difference?"

He nodded solemnly, but she just said something like "Men always side together" before shrugging off his opinion.

"Are there lessons for riding the chair lifts?" she went on, her eyes wide and curious. Before he could answer, she confided, "I never quite got the hang of it in Scotland. I fell off a couple of times trying to get on." Will smothered a smile when she added, "Fell getting off once too. Took out the next three chairloads with me."

"I'm sure the lift attendants will give you a hand," he managed to say, trying very hard not to laugh. It was a losing battle, though, because the image of Maggie anywhere near the slopes was akin to chaos unleashed.

Their drinks arrived and he sipped his slowly. He was thoroughly entertained by her mostly one-sided conversation, couldn't remember the last time he'd enjoyed himself more. Most of the things she said made absolutely no sense, but that didn't seem to bother her.

Every so often he caught her looking at him, and he'd say something to let her know he wasn't asleep.

He'd never been further from sleep in his entire life. She was fascinating—a mixture of sexuality and lunacy, and skittish enough to make him wonder if she knew about the sex part. She must have known, though, because she was looking at him with a kind of open curiosity that aroused him despite his intentions not to be aroused!

Maggie wished she could stop babbling, but her tongue was on a roll and she didn't know how to stop it. He wasn't bored, she knew. He wasn't the type of man to tolerate boredom. Maybe he really enjoyed the prattle of her monologue, although she couldn't imagine how anyone could stand the maze of non sequiturs and inane stories she'd invented especially for this night.

She licked her lips and watched as his gaze followed the movement. Will Jackson's deep-set blue-gray eyes were rapidly convincing her that his enjoyment wasn't a figment of her imagination. Even more, he was *sexually* interested!

She was scared to death.

Taking a deep breath, she gulped back the panic and threw out a line that was guaranteed to slacken the pace. "I like your tie."

"My tie?" He looked at her, then at the tie, then back at her again. "My tie?" he repeated.

"You don't see many men who can wear one and not look like they're choking," she said, secretly amused at his dazed expression. "Was it a gift or did you find it yourself?" Without giving him a chance to respond, she continued. "Personally, I hope you bought it yourself because that means it reflects your personality. Kind of like the car you drive, you know?"

Will shook his head in disbelief. He'd managed to follow her train of thought and that disturbed him. "I drive a four by four," he said.

"Four by four? That makes sixteen wheels—a semi, I suppose! Odd, I would have pegged you for one of those rugged Jeeps you see in the commercials on TV. You know, the ones that go charging across streams or climbing mountains of rock." Maggie knew perfectly well what a four by four was, but it was too good of an opportunity to let pass. Then she tried to look confused, wrinkling her brow and chewing delicately on her lip, feigning disappointment. "It's strange, though."

"What's strange?" Will could have answered that question several ways himself. He wanted to hear what she thought was strange.

"The tie, of course," she said. "It's not at all the kind of thing I'd imagine a truck driver would wear—silk and all, not that I've spent much time thinking about it. But if someone had asked me to pick out a tie for a truck driver, I'd probably go for something a bit more practical, rayon or maybe one of those ribbed knits that look so terrific with madras shirts." She smiled brightly, telling him with her expression that she was proud of him for having the taste to pick out a silk tie. Surprised, but proud. "I guess that shows how much I don't know about truck drivers. You probably make pretty good money hauling stuff around if you can afford silk ties."

His mouth was gaping open, but he couldn't help it. The things she was saying were so incredibly off the wall! He stared at her as she lifted her wineglass for a small sip, and finally managed to pull his jaw back up before she remarked on it.

"Semis have eighteen wheels, I think," he said, getting the facts straightened out . . . although he didn't know why he bothered.

He should have known this would confuse her.

"So how come yours has sixteen?" she asked.

"It doesn't have sixteen. It has four." He drained the last of his drink in one gulp, plunked the glass back on the table, and tried to explain. "I drive a four by four—that means a four-wheel-drive truck, just like those you were talking about, on TV."

She managed to look a little peeved. "How can you call yourself a truck driver if you've only got four wheels to your name?"

"I didn't say I was a truck driver," he said wearily. "You said I was a truck driver."

"Then what *do* you do?" she asked, pleased with her exasperated tone, which made it seem like all this talk about truck drivers was deliberate subterfuge on his part.

"I'm in business."

"Truck drivers are in business."

Will sighed. Apparently, nothing but an abbreviated résumé would put an end to this. "I have a variety of interests. Mostly, though, I spend my time working in real estate."

"So why didn't you just say so, instead of making me think you were a truck driver?"

"What's wrong with being a truck driver?" he asked instead, thinking that if he could turn the tables he might get through this without looking like a complete idiot.

"Nothing's wrong with being a truck driver," she said earnestly, "but pretending to be one is another matter altogether. Why, I might have a thing about truck drivers and you'd use it to make up to me and then what would I feel like when I found out the truth?"

"I'm not a truck driver," he said with a tone of finality that dared her to disagree.

"Good." Maggie let her smile broaden, confident she had a handle on the rhythm of their circuitous dialogue. It was hard work, taking his words and twisting them to make it seem she didn't have a firm grasp on much of anything.

From the look of things, Will was as confused as she pretended to be.

Will tried not to show his relief when she changed the subject and asked him about what it was like living in Tahoe. He talked with only half his attention on what he was saying. The other half concentrated on her eyes as she listened, savoring the way they sparkled in the reflection of the candle that flickered between them.

Couples were dancing on a tiny parquet floor in the corner. The soft music encouraged a bonding of the most civilized persuasion. It was a simple dance, each partner holding the other and moving in a rhythm that was considered suitable to the environment—other people watching and a lack of privacy.

Will didn't think about it. He just stood and pulled her up beside him, breathing a sigh of gratitude when she followed without hesitation to that corner where he could touch her and not have to apologize for it. He wanted her close, totally ignoring how tiny she was. He needed to see if she fit into his arms. He must have known the answer to that, though, because it was like déjà vu when she melted into his embrace, her arms lifting to wrap around his neck.

He moved slowly to the music and memorized the feel of her. It would most likely be the only chance he ever got.

"Are you coming inside, or are you going to stay out there all night?"

Without turning to face him, Maggie said she rather thought she'd stay where she was. The sliding door closed behind her and she listened hard. If she heard the door to the hallway slam shut, she could go back inside her room before she turned into an ice cube. Otherwise . . . *Sculpture of a Woman Who Changed Her Mind,* she imagined the caption in the guidebook would read, and the tourists would stare at her frozen figure until they too, began to freeze.

Shivering relentlessly in the subfreezing environment of the balcony off her room, Maggie hugged herself with arms that couldn't spare her any warmth. They were just as cold as the rest of her. She wished she'd had the sense to bring her coat with her, but knew she'd stand out there all night rather than go back inside. Now, with only a thin sweater and slacks to protect her from the elements, she figured her chances of surviving even another five minutes were extremely poor.

Still, it was better than facing the man she'd left in the hotel room behind her.

She heard the sliding door again and wondered if she should latch onto the railing if he tried to drag her back inside. Not that it would do her any good to resist. Will was bigger and stronger and a lot less frozen than she was. Besides, she doubted her stiffening fingers could latch onto anything at the moment. She dumped thoughts of any physical resistance and was getting ready for some verbal sparring, when something warm and soft enveloped her shoulders.

It took a couple of seconds; her thought processes were slowed thanks to her cooling blood running sluggishly to her brain. "My coat?" she finally said, turning to him as he ducked back inside to collect the two brandy snifters he'd left on the table.

"Your coat," he said. He waited until she'd pushed her arms into the downy thick sleeves, then handed her one of the drinks. He saluted her with his own before downing a healthy gulp. He wasn't dressed for standing under the stars in spring, but he'd be damned if he'd chase all the way back downstairs for the overcoat he'd left at reception.

He knew Maggie wouldn't let him back into her room, no matter how quick he was.

So he stayed, because he wanted to know why the woman who'd invited him to her room was suddenly afraid to go through with it.

Maggie cautiously sipped her cognac. The fiery liquid warmed her insides as the coat took the edge off the outer chill. She looked sideways at the man leaning against the terrace railing and wondered why he was still there.

"Cold feet?" he asked.

She slipped back into her Bambi Bubblehead character with an ease that worried her. "Not yet," she said, looking down at her leather shoes. "But I'm sure they'll be the next to go."

Will laughed aloud. He couldn't stop himself. Then he tried again. "That's not what I meant, Maggie. I was asking why you're hiding out here on the balcony."

"Then you should have said so," she snapped, and took another sip of cognac without meeting his eyes. She'd invited him to her room and now she was too chicken to do anything about it. How on earth had she gotten into this mess?

"I'll try to be more direct," he promised, watching her carefully. He didn't want to frighten her; she was nervous enough already. "I think I'd like to know why you're hiding out here, if you wouldn't mind explaining it to me. You invited me to your room with the promise of making love and I'm still waiting."

"I didn't promise anything," she retorted, but that

wasn't true. *I want to make love with you,* she'd whispered into his ear, and she'd meant it. They'd spent nearly an hour dancing, holding each other, learning so much and hiding so little. Well, perhaps she had left out one or two minor points. Such as who was the real woman inside the caricature that had attracted him in the first place.

For an hour she'd charmed and vamped as he'd held her more closely, more intimately than seemed decent. Yet she knew he was a decent man. She'd babbled and blithered, making him laugh at her, with her, seducing him with the sensual dingbat role she'd copied to perfection and hiding her disappointment that he believed it all.

"Shall I go?" Will asked, and hoped she wouldn't say yes. He was curious about her sudden reluctance, unwilling to leave her without finding out why she'd changed her mind. It was a bit of a mystery, and he wondered what had happened to the delightfully provocative woman she'd been earlier. That she was slightly off center didn't bother him, although she'd shown flashes of sanity that were strangely comforting, short moments in which she seemed to pause for a breath, as if to recharge for another round of madness.

He'd never met anyone quite like her, and was absolutely certain he never would again. He couldn't decide if that was good or bad, but he didn't worry about it. After tonight he'd never see her again, and whatever happened between them would be a memory, nothing more.

He repeated his question when she didn't seem to have heard. "Maggie, do you want me to go?"

She'd heard him the first time and now she knew she must say something, anything that would keep him with her. But she was irritated with herself. It wasn't his fault she'd lost her nerve. She looked up and saw the gently amused expression on his face, and in that moment, she knew he understood.

"I'm scared," she said softly.

"I know."

That gave her courage like nothing else he could have said or done. Perhaps she'd be able to go through with it after all. Maggie put aside any thoughts of reticence and decided that getting it out into the open was the best strategy. "I've never done anything like this before."

"Neither have I," he said.

Three

"Well, that really tears it!"

Her nervousness instantly quelled by frustration, Maggie met his dumbfounded stare. "What am I supposed to do now?" she demanded. "Give lessons?"

"Excuse me?" Will swallowed hard and tried to figure out what she was talking about.

"When I invited you up here, I was under the impression you'd done this before!"

"I don't underst—"

She cut him off with a frustrated growl. "Of all the men in all the bars around Lake Tahoe, I end up with a virgin. Can't beat that for luck, can you?"

Will jerked in astonishment, spilling the rest of his cognac onto the icy planks at their feet. So that's what she was riled about. He would have laughed if she hadn't been so damned upset.

"That's not what I—" he began.

"How am I supposed to get any useful feedback from you?" she muttered, scowling up at him.

"Feedback?"

"Should have known a man pretending to be a truck driver wouldn't get me anywhere."

"I didn't pretend to be a truck dri—"

She interrupted, again. "A *virgin* truck driver! Who'd believe it?"

"I didn't say I was a virgin!"

"You said—"

He covered her mouth with his free hand. "Hush, Maggie," he said mildly, and waited until she stood still. He wasn't fooled by her acquiescence, though. Her eyes were shooting silver-green sparks all over him.

The shimmering beauty of those sparks touched his soul in a way he had never known before. Even in her anger, she made him want to laugh for the pleasure of just being with her.

He made a wise decision not to laugh.

"I said, or I meant to say, that I've never slept with a woman I've only just met."

Above the solid muzzle of his hand, her eyes rolled in disbelief. He elaborated. "I make it a rule to avoid one-night stands. I prefer relationships, where sex is a part of the whole and not simply the beginning and end."

Her lips moved against his palm, the sensation definitely erotic from his standpoint and functional from hers. She had something to say. Regretfully, he dropped his hand to his side.

"I don't *want* a relationship!" she said in a rush. "I could have gotten that at home if I wanted it. Which I don't."

"I'm not offering one," he said gently.

Silly to feel disappointed, Maggie told herself.

"You're making an exception to your rule tonight?" she asked anxiously.

"I had thought so," he murmured, "but it seems we've lost the mood, if you don't mind me saying so." And then, there was the matter of virgin territory. Will hadn't bargained for that complication.

He didn't want anything to do with her if that was the case. He had to find out.

"As long as we've come this far, though," he said,

"what exactly did *you* mean when you said you'd never done this before?"

Fair's fair, Maggie admitted silently. Still, it took several deep breaths before she could get it out.

"Same thing as you, more or less," she said hesitantly. "I've never been picked up by a stranger in a bar."

"You picked me up," he pointed out.

She shrugged, remembering her airhead alter ego. "Whatever. If it's important to you, you can tell your friends downstairs I did it. I don't want to ruin your reputation."

Will couldn't stop the chuckle. "I don't think you'll have to tell anyone anything. You were just a little obvious."

She smothered a groan of embarrassment, grateful the dark night hid the flush creeping up her face. "That takes care of that, then," she said breezily.

"Not really." Lifting her chin with a single finger, he held her gaze with his own. "Are you a virgin, Maggie? Yes or no."

She thought it would make a better impression if she didn't melt under the electric warmth of his touch, so she forced a giggle and a grin. "Don't be a goose! Imagining for the moment that I'd reached the age of thirty-one with my virginity intact, would I be likely to, er, surrender it to a man I hardly know?"

"Is that a no?"

She nodded her head, the short fall of dark and light gold silk shivering in the moonlight, brushing his fingers. He believed her.

And he wanted her. In that wanting, he forgot all about the other question he'd meant to ask, particularly the one about "feedback." Instead, he took a single step back and studied the small woman looking up at him. How, he wondered, did he go about recapturing the exquisitely sensual mood between them without scaring her off?

Maggie sighed and stared into eyes that were studying her with speculative detachment. He was thinking how best to leave, she realized, and berated herself for letting her nerves get the best of her. He was the stuff out of which dreams were made—gorgeous, sensitive . . . *discriminating.*

She'd messed up big time.

If he left her now, she'd have to start all over again tomorrow night with someone else, another man who couldn't possibly make her feel the things Will could with just a look, a touch . . . a slow dance that made her heart race and her imagination soar.

The erotic aura had only lasted until they'd mounted the stairs to her room, though. She'd made the mistake of walking ahead of him, slipping her fingers from his grasp so she could get there first and put the key in the lock before he saw her shaking hands.

Nerves had taken over once his touch wasn't there to reassure her, to warm her. She'd walked straight past the bed and out onto the balcony without even stopping to see if he followed.

From the disco below a heavy Latin beat pulsed through the walls and windows, not so much drifting to the couple on the balcony as it thrust itself upon them. It was loud and obnoxious in the cold, thin air, but it gave her an idea.

"We could dance again," she said. She swayed to the music as it invaded her senses, shyly hoping he'd take the incentive and pull her into his arms.

"Isn't it a bit fast?" he asked, a corner of his mouth lifting as he realized their roles had changed. She wanted him to take charge, set the pace. It was a side of her she hadn't shown him earlier, a vulnerability that was more real than anything he'd seen in her before. Perhaps the flatlands were she lived weren't so far away after all.

"If you don't want to dance, we could have another drink," she added, a slightly desperate note coloring her tone. She looked up into his face. "If you touch me, I know I'll be okay."

"Like this?" he asked. Holding her gaze with his, he slipped his hand into the deep pocket of her coat, where she'd shoved hers. He let the small contact be their only one, and felt his desire for her kindle to a sizzling heat.

Maggie nodded and turned her palm outward so she could curl her fingers into his. It felt so right, she was amazed to realize. So perfect. And it didn't matter if her hand was clammy or sweaty or frozen. Will wouldn't care about things like that. Swallowing hard because it was such a beautiful feeling, she took a deep breath and asked him if he was still thinking of leaving.

"No," he said.

She followed him inside, stepping carefully since it was kind of hard to walk with their hands still joined inside the pocket of her coat. They slipped precariously on the balcony floor as he shoved open the door with his elbow, the snifter occupying his other hand. Once inside, he put it and hers down, then reached behind her to close the door. He must have noticed the cold more than she had, she mused, wearing only a shirt beneath his corduroy jacket.

She felt like she was burning up.

Inside, the ambitious Latin beat was a muted, sensual throb that was a rhythmic accompaniment to her pounding heart. His hand didn't leave hers, and she knew it was because he understood her need to feel his assurance. He led her slowly around the room, snapping off the overhead lights, flicking on the one beside the bed, and chiding her with his eyes when she opened her mouth to object. The words died in her throat when she saw the raw desire in his gaze . . . and she knew she'd do whatever he asked. It would be worth it to be able to keep it with her forever, the memory of how he looked at her in that moment.

Even if nothing more intimate occurred between them that night, it would be enough to remember he'd wanted her more than she'd ever dreamed a man could.

Slowly, he raised their joined hands from the depths of her pocket, lifting them until he could see their tangled fingers. He studied them from several angles, flexing and straightening his grip but not once letting go. When he was finished, his eyes met hers. He smiled at her puzzled expression.

"We fit," he said with a touch of surprise in his voice. "You're so little, I'd have thought I'd be too big. But I was wrong, and I can't figure out why."

"I'm five feet three," she said.

"No you're not." He chuckled when she had the grace to blush. "I'm just surprised at how well we fit, that's all. I'm a big man, about a foot taller than you. But it doesn't seem to matter. I knew it when we danced. And now our hands. They don't look odd at all."

Maggie hadn't thought of him as a particularly big man, but then most everyone was bigger than she. It hadn't occurred to her that it might bother him. Just as she was getting set to worry about it, he said something that made her heart pound almost painfully.

"I'm going to take your clothes off now, Maggie," he said softly, "so you can either give me your lips and let me get to know your mouth . . . or you can watch, if you like." He turned her a little until she could see their reflections in the dresser mirror. His free hand lifted to her shoulder and he began to push the coat aside, slowly, steadily, until her arm was suddenly free.

She was fully clothed, with a heavy winter parka half-on, half-off, and she'd never felt more naked in her life. Maggie shut her eyes, overwhelmed by the things he made her feel with so little effort. When his mouth brushed hers, she was unable to prevent the spasm that made her fingers clench around his.

She held her breath until his lips settled upon hers and he slowly increased the pressure. It was exquisite to feel his hard, masculine mouth, sheer heaven when he pressed harder, opening her beneath him until whatever breath she took was from him. He didn't move, not for the longest time, a second . . . an eternity. He was waiting for something, *waiting for her!* she realized.

Carefully, cautiously, she drew her tongue along the rim of their clinging lips, tracing where they were joined. It was new and scary and so incredibly erotic, she would have known he liked it even if she hadn't heard his groan of approval.

That was only the beginning.

He never let go of her, not then, not later. The fingers that were so tightly entwined parted, but his mouth held hers as he slowly tugged off her coat. Again he took her hand, showing her how easily he could remove her clothes with only one set of extremely dexterous fingers. He kissed away her blushes when she was naked and he wasn't, then shifted his grip from one hand to the other as he shed his own clothing.

He held her close when she began to shiver, not from the cold but from excitement. He knew that, she realized, because the way he embraced her wasn't meant to warm but to arouse. Between kisses, he whispered tantalizing promises into her ears, thrilled her with his hands that trembled ever so slightly, pleasured her and, in return, taught her what pleasured him.

She discovered the rippling strength of his shoulders and the smooth contours of his chest, where she delighted in finding exactly three hairs and no more! They were gray hairs and she giggled, asking if he was as old as he looked. He told her he was old enough, and did she want to see his driver's license?

She wanted to hear it from him. She demanded his age. He refused, and she accused him of unreasonable vanity. He dared her to force it out of him. She stroked and tickled and caressed until he surrendered in a blaze of passion. Gasping for breath, he admitted he was forty, then he captured her hands and began to repay the sensual punishment.

For a moment, he did nothing . . . nothing except look at her.

Maggie had to try very hard not to squirm under the intensity of his gaze. A trace of embarrassment tinted her skin, but she felt excitement too, and that easily overwhelmed any other response. His gaze traveled over her, almost touching her. . . . She wished he would touch her!

And then he did.

Lightly, with the fingers of just one hand because the other was occupied making sure she didn't interfere, he drew a circle around her kneecap. She gasped. He smiled, and did it again.

So little, so exciting.

Will wanted to turn her gasps into moans. He tucked his hand between her legs, urging her to flex one knee as he drew that leg up and apart from the other. The inside of her thighs was exposed, and he wasted no time discovering the increasingly satiny texture as his hand slid upward toward the tight blond curls between her legs.

His caress was slow, steadily approaching the part of her that was moist and open to his touch. A soft moan left her lips, but he wanted more.

He opened his mouth on the smooth flesh beside his hand, and she cried aloud.

His fingers invaded the wet, honeyed nest and his mouth followed. Nipping softly, tasting the magic that was Maggie, he tested her responses, extracting from her the moans he'd sought.

And he discovered that his own excitement was equal to hers.

Later, when they'd collapsed onto their backs on the bed, breathing hard and exquisitely satisfied, she asked what was wrong with being forty. He smirked and told her he had lots of secrets she could torture out of him.

Maggie had never known laughter like this before, certainly never in bed, and she had the nerve to ask if he was having as much fun as she. "Can't you tell?" he said, then changed the mood with a very serious caress.

The cool sheet at her back was soon heated from her passionate response, the other tangled at their feet where they had shoved it out of the way. Maggie became the wanton she'd never been, taking chances, daring to do whatever she pleased because he encouraged her, pushed her. Her hair was damp with sweat and he didn't care, his lips nuzzling the wet strands as he teased her about her insatiable appetite . . . and would she please hand him another of those packets she'd stored in the bedside drawer? He wanted her, again, and didn't think he'd be able to wait much longer.

She'd blushed hotly when she'd first told him about the protection she'd bought, but he'd smiled and told her she'd "done good." She knew he meant it.

Maggie laughed with him, struggling with nearly hysterical tears as he tried something particularly acrobatic and failed. She caught her breath helplessly when he got back at her for her teasing, his sensual retaliation broadening her sexual experience as well as her vocabulary.

He took her to the brink, to a place she'd never truly seen before, and he sent her over the edge again and again . . . until she lost forever the doubts that had brought her to him.

More than once that night Will followed her sensual path, joining her in an erotic abandonment he'd never experienced with another woman.

In the meager light of winter's dawn, more asleep than awake, he reached for her again and caressed her gently . . . firmly. She murmured something soft and unintelligible, but he brushed aside her words with kisses and coaxed her thighs open. He eased into her wet warmth and began a slow rhythm that he knew would soon have her writhing beneath him—just as he knew her eyes would open and lock with his seconds before she was overwhelmed by the climax that seemed to surprise her every time it happened.

He knew so much about her already, startling for the few hours they'd spent together. It should have bothered him, this naturalness with which they shared life's greatest intimacy, but it didn't. He could only think about what more he wanted to learn, to share.

For now, though, he only wanted to see it again—the surprise . . . the joy. His hands reached back to urge her thighs higher around him, closer. Raised on his forearms so that he could watch, he joined with her as she soared to the heights of feeling. Together, without any sense of beginning or end, they opened their souls to a mind-shattering fulfillment that neither could have possibly anticipated or planned.

Making love with Maggie was as natural to him as breathing.

He could do it without thinking.

When Maggie awoke she knew where she was, who she was with, and precisely what they'd done together.

She grinned and snuggled closer to the warm, masculine chest that rose and fell at even intervals. Sex with Will had been passionate, wild, *sensational.* She deliberately called it sex, shying away from the phrase *making love.*

Something inside of her clutched as she considered the implications of that often misused euphemism, but she put it down to an empty stomach.

Even Maggie knew you could only make love if your heart was involved. A one-night stand, Will had called it. She owed him a big enough debt already without mangling the morning after with hints of emotion. Making love was for lovers; sex was for consenting adults.

And terrific sex it had been.

You're sexless and inhibited and cold. She'd believed her ex-husband, perhaps not the first time or the second, but certainly by the time Charles had said it for months on end the stark reality had begun to sink in.

He hadn't said anything in the beginning years of their marriage, although Maggie had known their intimate life was a long way from satisfactory. When she'd tried to talk with him about their problems, he'd refused. More accurately, she realized later, he'd deliberately put her off. He had waited until he was out of school and had his degree—the degree she had quit her own studies to help him attain.

He'd waited until he passed the bar exam, letting her go on supporting him, waiting tables some nights and most days. He'd waited until he had the job of his dreams with a firm that was the cream of the crop.

Then he'd told her why she didn't like sex. It wasn't his fault, he'd explained. She simply wasn't any good at it.

Four years to the day after she'd married him, Charles walked out of her life and into the arms of a woman he claimed he loved. A woman who knew how to please a man, he gloated. She was served with divorce papers within a week.

While she might have been foolish enough to love Charles, Maggie had consoled herself, at least there was another mistake she had *not* made.

She'd never shown him her journal . . . her dreams.

Over the next few years those dreams had given her strength as the fantasies of her mind pushed the edge of reality, until she'd finally had to separate fact from fiction.

Her journal was fact.

Her stories were fiction.

And her dream of becoming a writer was a secret she shared with no one. To Maggie's way of thinking, it would be as ridiculous as saying "When I grow up, I want to be a princess. Or a rock star."

Ridiculous. Dreams didn't pay the bills.

Her thoughts flitted back to her ex-husband's accusations . . . and the sure knowledge that they had been no more than an excuse for his own lack of expertise.

Maggie rubbed her cheek against Will's chest, almost purring her contentment. Charles had never made love to her, she realized now as she lay warm and content in Will's embrace.

Charles hadn't known how.

Her lips curved upward in sleep. In the gray light of early morning, Will studied Maggie with a nagging sense of disquiet.

She felt good in his arms. She looked as though she

belonged there. The sensual pleasures of the night had left him sated and content. Making love with Maggie put to shame any previous experience of a sexual nature. What's more, he'd savored every minute of the laughter and the talk that flowed around and in between the lovemaking.

He could imagine waking up to her every morning for the rest of his life.

That was the disquieting part. Will didn't intend to share his life with anyone. It was a matter of principle: Marriage was the first inevitable step to divorce. He'd seen enough of those to last him a lifetime.

Not even Casey's apparently successful marriage could change his opinion. It was wishful thinking to believe that Harriet and Casey would be as happy in five years as they were now.

The statistics were against them.

Staring down at the sleeping blonde in his arms, Will found himself wondering if the risks were worth it. Keeping Maggie close was a strangely appealing temptation.

He watched her eyelids flutter open. The eyes were clouded with sleep, and he waited a long moment for them to focus. He looked closely for any signs of the return of the previous night's nervousness.

All he saw was a reflection of the same contentment he was feeling.

"Good morning," he said, and dropped a kiss on her forehead.

"Hello."

"Do you feel as good as you look?"

Maggie gave herself a minute to think about it, because the first thought that popped into her mind was definitely not what she was supposed to say. *I want to be with you forever.* That wasn't something he wanted to hear. She knew that.

You gave me my life. Much too heavy for the morning after, even if it was true. Will had given her what her husband had stolen. The harsh words that had clung to her in the years since her divorce faded into insignificance. She had Will to thank for that.

She need never doubt again that she was capable of pleasing a man. She had pleased Will the previous night. He'd told her so with words, with tender caresses . . . with responses so passionate, she'd been drawn into the whirlwind of his excitement time and time again.

A one-night stand, he'd termed it. If ever there was a time that she should stick to the rules, this was it. Will deserved no less.

"I feel terrific," she said slowly, drawing out the words as she slipped from his embrace and stretched her arms high above her head. She smiled. "Good sex *always* makes me feel like a new woman." Closing her eyes because she was afraid their expression would reveal her distaste for what she'd just said, she forced a yawn and waited for his response.

She sensed the stiffening of his body even though they were no longer touching. He wasn't pleased, she realized. That stumped her.

"I thought you said you didn't make a habit of this."

Her eyes flew open. "I said I didn't pick up men in bars," she said evenly. "I never said I didn't fool around once in a while." Quickly, so that he wouldn't see the blush that accompanied the lie, she turned away and crawled off the bed. She looked for a robe, a towel, anything that would shield her naked body from his gaze. She couldn't race for the security of the bathroom because she wasn't supposed to be embarrassed.

Will countered his surge of temper with the realization that Maggie was lying. The woman he'd made love to the previous night hadn't been experienced. He'd swear to that. She'd barely known the basics, until he'd taught her. He had to admit she'd learned quickly, and her delight with each new sensation had increased his own. Her passionate responses had surprised her, though. She couldn't have faked either—the response *or* the surprise.

She'd acted as though her first climax was just that: her first climax . . . *ever*.

She was lying about fooling around. He knew it. He wondered if he'd ever find out why. It didn't matter, he told himself. Another hour, maybe two, and he'd be out of her life forever.

He wasn't ready to leave yet.

Sitting up, he pushed away the covers and watched thoughtfully as Maggie moved around the room. She tugged open a bureau drawer, then walked over to the closet. Her body was flushed under his stare, another clue that she wasn't nearly as blasé as she pretended. Will felt his own body respond in a totally normal way as he remembered the incredibly erotic sensation of her nipples hardening under his mouth. And the satiny texture of her inner thighs, opening wide for his touch, closing tightly around him as he sheathed himself in the wet heat of her body.

He wanted her again.

"What are you looking for?" he asked softly.

Maggie almost tore the silk bathrobe from its hanger. "Found it," she mumbled, pushing her arms into the sleeves. She tied the belt before she dared to glance at him.

The look in his eyes was hot and sexy. Her gaze slid down his chest to the hard arousal jutting out from a nest of dark curls. When her gaze flew back to his face, she saw one corner of his mouth lift as a red flush climbed to her cheeks. She shivered beneath the flimsy robe, felt her sensitized nipples harden and push against the silk. "I don't have another robe for you. . . ."

"I don't need one," he said, his gaze fixed on her breasts. "Neither do you. Take it off and come back to bed."

Maggie swallowed. Things were spinning out of control. She'd thought he'd be up and out of there in the middle of the night. But he'd stayed, sleeping with her, arousing her again and again . . . satisfying her with a determination that had nearly driven her mindless.

She hadn't expected him to want more. She hadn't known she was capable of feeling the same. She did, though. Her only problem was to hide the other things she was feeling.

"It's morning," she said, stalling.

"Sex is always exciting in the mornings," he said huskily. "But you know that, don't you?"

She flushed yet again and Will knew he hadn't misjudged her. Maggie might have made love to other men before—although he doubted if there was more than one or two in her past—but last night was the first time she'd enjoyed it.

"Come back to bed, Maggie. Or else . . ."

"Or else what?" she whispered, her gaze locked to his as she found herself sliding helplessly into the realms of pleasure so recently visited.

"Or else I'll have to come to you." He saw the rapid intake of breath that signaled her anticipation, and he reveled in it. Maggie was so wonderfully responsive. He wondered if he could possibly get enough of her in the few hours they had left.

Rising from the bed, he walked slowly toward her. "I can do that, if you like. Come to you. I haven't taken you standing up yet, have I? Or there's an armchair over there that might be interesting. What do you think, Maggie?"

He wasn't surprised when she didn't answer. He smiled as he reached her, put his lips near one ear, and began to whisper alternative suggestions if the other two didn't appeal.

A tiny cry escaped her when he told her that perhaps, time permitting, they'd try them all.

The sun was a ricochet of light on the pristine mountain slopes when Maggie slipped out of Will's arms. Quietly but with almost frantic haste, she washed her face, stroked her lashes with mascara, then scrambled into her ski clothes.

She left without waking him, quite a trick really,

considering the armful of boots and mittens and other miscellaneous gear.

It wasn't that she didn't know that she should at least say good-bye to the man who had given back to her so much of herself.

She just didn't think she could.

Four

Will was conscious one moment and reaching for Maggie the next. He came up empty. He contained his disappointment, thinking she might be in the bathroom.

In his gut, though, he knew she was gone. He couldn't feel her anywhere near.

He swung his feet to the floor and checked, just to be sure.

He was alone.

Her clothes were still there, the things she'd worn the night before exactly where they'd fallen when he'd peeled them from her body. His own were there too, wrinkled trousers on top of pink cashmere, his shirt somehow tangled in lacy straps of her teddy.

She hadn't even bothered to say good-bye.

He dressed, let himself out of a side door of the hotel, and drove home. He even went to work, just long enough to let his temper spark off every single member of his staff.

He'd wanted to kiss her good morning, taste her mouth one last time before they went their separate ways.

He felt like he'd been cheated, so he went looking for her.

Cruising the beginner slopes in search of Maggie, Will realized he didn't know what he was going to say when he caught up with her. That didn't stop him, though. It was enough that he'd have the last word.

That was until he began to hear the stories of her escapades. Then he just wanted to get her off the slopes before it was too late.

He tried to have the ski patrol yank her lift pass. They just laughed and said they could only do that if she was caught skiing out of control.

Will argued that from what he'd heard, skiing out of control would be a step up for Maggie.

She skied badly, not dangerously, they countered. It wasn't her fault she fell as often as she turned.

She was a menace, he insisted.

Accident prone, they rationalized. Not her fault at all. And as long as she stuck to beginner slopes, they didn't see any reason to spoil her fun.

Will didn't have any such scruples, but it was almost afternoon before he caught up with her.

His skis chattered across a patch of crusted snow as he made his way across the slope to where a small crowd had gathered around the scene of destruction. Through the small forest of colorful parkas and sweaters, flashes of turquoise confirmed his hunch. By the time he edged to a stop at the periphery of the crowd she was already standing.

So was the guy she'd run into.

Judging by the wide array of skis and poles, sunglasses and other miscellaneous gear scattered in the near vicinity, it had been one of her more spectacular accidents. It didn't have anything on the pileup she'd caused at the top of the chair lift, though. That one had taken the lift attendants ten minutes to straighten out.

She was lucky to be alive.

Will was pretty sure he was going to kill her . . . if the other guy didn't take care of that for him. It never occurred to him that it hadn't been Maggie's fault. He'd been hearing accounts of the "Turquoise Terror" almost from the moment he'd started looking for her.

His stomach gradually unclenched as she shook snow out of her pockets and gloves. Eyes hidden behind the mirrored lenses of his sunglasses, he scooted close enough to listen.

". . . didn't know you were going to go that way," she was saying. "Imagine my surprise when you zigged instead of zagged."

The man stared at her as though she was from outer space. "Why didn't you just turn?" he asked.

She shrugged. "I did." She pointed to a spot about fifty feet uphill. "I hadn't planned on doing another quite so soon."

She made it sound as though the other skier had messed her up on purpose.

He flushed and apologized. Maggie smiled and said not to worry, no harm done. Will shook his head in disbelief.

She'd gotten away with it again.

Without any broken bones to hold their interest, the crowd drifted away from the multiple sitzmarks. The male half of the accident stepped into his skis with a swiftness that betrayed his anxiousness to escape. He didn't even bother to brush off the snow that clumped on his sweater but headed straight down the hill without turning or checking his speed. He glanced over his shoulder just once, as though to assure himself he wasn't being followed.

That didn't seem to be a problem. Maggie put herself together much more slowly than she fell apart.

Will watched as she gathered her equipment and began the tedious process of putting on her skis mid-slope. He kept silent as she conscientiously knocked the snow off the bottom of her boot with her pole, then tried to maintain her balance without putting her foot back onto the slope—all of this necessary if she was going to get the boot back into the bindings. One false step and she'd have to start all over again.

She got lucky. The binding snapped into place, securing her boot to the ski. Digging one pole into the hill, Maggie went to work on the other boot—the downhill one. It was a precarious position, one that was unbalanced and just plain contrary to the laws of physics.

Any fool knew better than to put on the uphill ski first. Will could have told her that, but her back was turned and he needed those precious seconds before discovery to try to put a damper on his temper.

Maggie struggled to knock the snow from the bottom of her boot without losing her balance. It was a maneuver doomed for failure, and he waited patiently for the inevitable.

Three seconds later she let out a little scream as she tipped over, falling face first into the snow, her body pointing down the gentle slope. Under the slight pressure, her uphill ski popped off—just as it was supposed to. Will was grateful that Scott hadn't taken Maggie's self-proclaimed "advanced-intermediate" boast at face value, because then the bindings would have been tighter and might not have been so willing to part company with her boot, thereby risking a broken leg. Thanks to Scott's astute estimation of Maggie's nonexistent skills, everything was as it should be.

"Maggie?" Will said inquiringly.

Her head lifted and she said, "Will?" as though she couldn't believe her bad luck.

"Mmm-hmm."

She buried her face in the snow.

He wondered if she could breathe like that. "Are you ready to call it quits yet?"

The last word he'd been so intent upon would have to wait for another day.

She growled and beat her gloved fist against the hill.

"Come on, Maggie," he coaxed, digging his poles firmly into the snowpack and stepping out of his own skis. "If you don't get up, your mascara will run."

She lifted her head a couple of inches and muttered, "Go 'way!"

"Can't," he said as he circled her prone body and knelt down just inches from her face. "The ski patrol already knows I'm looking for you. If I leave you here like this, they'll cite me for littering the slope."

"Stuff the ski patrol," she said clearly. "They thought I was joking when I asked if I could hop a ride on one of their sleds."

"You did?"

She nodded, then lifted her face just enough to squint up at him. "Can't figure any other way to get off this damn mountain."

"You mean you've been trying to get to the bottom all this time?" he asked incredulously.

She nodded again, and her forehead plunked back onto the snow. Will thought he heard a bit of sniffling in the background.

His heart lurched at her complete vulnerability. "Are you tired, love?" he asked gently.

She definitely sniffled and mumbled something that passed for yes.

"Hungry too, I'll bet," he said.

She groaned.

"Do you want me to help you?"

This time it was just a touch clearer. "Yes, please."

Will wasted no time. Reaching up the hill, he grabbed her by the thighs and slid her legs around. When her feet were headed downhill instead of up, he helped her cross one heavy boot over the other and, voilà, the rest of her body followed suit. She was looking at the sky instead of the snow.

Her mascara was streaked every which way, her hair half-wet and filled with clumps of snow, her nose bright red, and she looked ready to cry. He swallowed hard against the lump in his own throat, wondering where his anger had gone . . . and when. It didn't seem fair, he thought, that she should be so lost and alone.

Shucking a glove, he dug in a pocket for a tissue and went to work on her face, thinking that if she looked better she'd feel better. With gentle strokes, he erased all signs of mascara, noticing as he did that her face was devoid of any other cosmetics. Quite a change from the evening before. As his long fingers pulled through her hair, digging out the snow and smoothing damp strands off her forehead, he wondered how she'd react if he told her she didn't need any makeup at all.

He decided to err on the side of caution and kept quiet.

Maggie suffered his ministrations in silence too, only opening her eyes when he finally stuck the tissue under her nose and told her to blow.

She blew. "When did you get here?" she asked as he stuffed the tissue back into his pocket.

"Postcrash," he said mildly, resting back on his elbows so that she wouldn't feel like she had to look at him. She must be embarrassed enough at being caught in this predicament without having to put up with the "I knew you couldn't ski" look on his face. But only an act of God could have changed his expression.

"I arrived," he added, "just as you were just explaining to that guy why the accident wasn't your fault."

She grimaced. "If I hadn't been so tired I might have missed him, even if he hadn't turned right there in front of me."

Still the other guy's fault, Will noticed. He grinned.

"So go back to the part where you can't seem to get off this mountain," he said. "Don't you have a map with you?"

She snorted. "Lots of good that did. Half the green slopes are closed for lack of snow, which means you can only get to the very bottom if you cut across parts of the blue ones. Or black ones. Heaven forbid!"

Green translated as beginner runs, blue for intermediate, black for advanced. Will nodded. "And you didn't want to cross a blue one?" He refused to even think of Maggie on a black one.

"Ski patrol told me they'd slap the cuffs on me if I even breathed on one," she said.

"And you were too proud to explain it to them."

"I only found out about the essential black and blue bits after they warned me off," she admitted with a defeated shrug. "That was right before I dropped my map from the chair lift."

"You couldn't get another one?"

"They're out." She pulled off her glove and scratched her nose. "So I asked one of the lift attendants which way was home."

"And he said . . ."

She scowled. "He had the nerve to tell me that the Turquoise Terror shouldn't give up so easily, and that the odds were five to one that I'd break something before the day was out."

Will couldn't stop the chuckle that erupted at the disgust in her voice.

"So what did you tell him?"

Maggie sighed heavily. "Oh, I don't remember exactly," she fudged, "but I think I asked if he'd be satisfied if I broke my skis over his head." She turned her head to look directly at Will and lifted an expressive eyebrow. "He was *not* amused."

Rolling her head back and forth on the snow, she whimpered theatrically. "Every time I get to the bottom of a run, it's a dead end and I have to get on another lift just to get out of there. You can only go down so far before you have to go up again. I've been going in circles all morning and haven't really been anywhere!"

"Sounds like you've had a bad day," he said.

She sat up and looked him square in the eye. "The guy who thought up the name Heavenly Valley had a malicious sense of humor. Skiers' Hell, *that's* what they should call this place."

Will swallowed a laugh and turned back to examine the view spread out before them. Lake Tahoe was enormous and calm and so blue that day, the sky seemed lackluster in comparison. The mountains that bordered the lake were elegant standards of what mountains were supposed to look like—rugged, majestic, and just plain awesome.

Skiers' Hell. He decided that perhaps Maggie had lost her perspective.

"What are you doing over on the California side in the first place?" he asked. Heavenly Valley bridged Nevada and California by virtue of a series of lifts and trails that were fairly simple for most skiers—those who knew where they were going and had at least basic training in the fundamentals of skiing.

"California?" Maggie exclaimed. "What happened to Nevada?" A sinking feeling in her stomach told her her troubles were only just beginning. She'd heard all about the black diamond run at the bottom of the California side of the resort from a talkative teen who had bravely shared a ride on a double chair with her earlier. *The Face,* they called it. It was the only way down in California, because the easier runs were lacking snow at those lower altitudes.

Damn!

"I can't ski *The Face,*" she wailed. "Even *if* I managed to get that far and *if* the ski patrol didn't catch me first, I'd still kill myself before I took the first turn!"

Will agreed. *The Face* was a challenge for the best of skiers. He wondered if she knew she could take the tram back to the bottom—once they reached the midpoint. He avoided telling her, though, thinking things couldn't possibly be as dismal as she made out. She couldn't be as bad as rumor said. He'd get her back to Nevada and down again without too much trouble.

Even if it was a lot of trouble, he was willing. He wanted a whole woman in his bed that night, not one who was broken and wounded. He flinched as the image of Maggie hurt made his heart fall into an erratic rhythm. He couldn't let it happen!

"I'm never going to see that beautiful lodge again," she said, feeling sorry for herself now, because she was tired and hungry and enormously intimidated by the stretch of slope beneath her—not to mention the one she couldn't even see yet!

"Never say never, Maggie," Will said.

"Easy for you to say," she shot back. "You can probably get down whenever you feel like it."

He took off his glove again and snagged her hand, warming it in his. "If you have such a defeatist attitude, you'll just make yourself miserable. Try being more optimistic."

"I'm already miserable," she said, "and I lost all my

optimism when a smart-aleck five-year-old in the lift line asked if he could hold my poles for me so I wouldn't drop them." She sniffled. "It reminded me of the boy scout helping the old lady across the street."

"Did you let him?" Will asked, carefully hiding his laughter.

She flashed him an irritated look. "Of course I did. I'm inept, not stupid."

Inept. He puzzled over her surprising choice of words and then forgot it. "I might be able to get you out of here," he said lightly, turning his head to catch her gaze. "For a price."

"How much?" she asked with a touch of desperation. "Never mind. I don't care what it costs. Just get me off this mountain before I turn into a snowball."

His smile lasted only as long as it took him to remember that the price he planned to extract would be of value only if he managed to get both of them down without mishap.

He wondered if the ski patrol would be amenable to a bribe in exchange for the use of a sled.

It took ten minutes to get her brushed off, zipped up, and ready for action.

"All set?" he asked.

Maggie looked down the quarter mile of hideously sheer slope that disappeared over the crest of a hill and gulped. "I don't remember the mountains in Scotland ever being this steep. Are you sure I didn't somehow end up on an advanced slope?"

"Hardly." Will spared a cursory glance at the nearly flat stretch of hill and remembered to be kind. "It's just because we're up so high," he said. "It'll feel better once we get into the trees and you can't see so far."

She snorted in disbelief and stayed rooted to the spot.

"Do you know how to snowplow?"

"Is that anything like the twist?" Maggie thought it was time to throw in a touch of Bambi Bubblehead,

something she'd been too miserable to worry about
since finding herself trapped in the maze of slopes.

She felt much better now that Will was in charge.

He shook his head in resigned despair and assumed
the position. She glared at him when she saw how
easily he organized his skis into the wedge shape she
hadn't yet mastered.

Mastered! She giggled silently. She hadn't even got
the basics down, much less mastered anything.

"Why don't we just walk," she suggested. "I'm getting
awfully tired of falling down."

"You're too tired to walk. We'll be down in no time if
we ski."

"*You* might ski down," she snapped. "*I* usually just
slide on my butt until I run into somebody."

"If you stay behind me and turn where I turn, you'll
be okay," he said patiently, his knees already aching
from the unfamiliar strain. He hadn't used the snowplow since he was a kid and just learning to ski.

He'd never hear the end of it if anyone spotted him.

"Aren't you afraid I'll run into you?" she asked,
grunting as she lifted the heavy skis into position.

"No," he lied.

"This hurts my hips," she yelled, digging her poles
into the snow and shoving as Will began to slide across
the hill.

He looked back and said, "Don't spread 'em so wide.
Get the tips of your skis together."

"The stupid skis cross when I do that," she shouted,
covering the slope an inch at a time. "Do you think they
rented me two left skis?"

He turned and passed below her. "You're not good
enough to know the difference," he said smartly.

He turned again. "Bend your knees."

She squatted.

"Not so far." He passed her again, turned again.
Maggie wasn't even halfway across the slope.

"Tuck in your tush, Maggie. You don't want your
center of gravity hanging out behind you."

"Who says I don't? I'd rather fall on my butt than my face any day."

"You won't fall if you do what I tell you."

Maggie knew a lie when she heard one, and was careful to keep her center of gravity where she'd need it.

"Now turn just where I did."

"That's on a lump," she protested.

"A mogul, not a lump. And it's a baby one, nothing to worry about." He stopped to watch as she approached the lump.

She gestured wildly with her pole, slowly inching past the designated lump. "I'm going to go over there where it's flat."

"No!" He did another quick turn, inverting the snowplow until the tracks he made resembled a herringbone. Expertly striding up the gentle slope, he said, "Don't try to turn on that flat bit. It's too crusty. Maggie, no! You'll fall . . ." His voice trailed off as she hit the icy crust and lost whatever pretense of control she'd had.

The wedge of her snowplow widened, her arms flew upward, and her tush smacked hard on the snow. Will winced as he thought about what that position did to her hips. He watched as she slid the length of the ice patch, about twenty feet.

Only twenty feet. He sighed. It was going to take all day getting Maggie off this mountain. Directing his skis down, he bent his knees slightly and let gravity take him to a point just below the tips of her skis.

"If I'd listened to you, I'd have fallen on my face," she said matter-of-factly.

"If you'd listened to me, you wouldn't have fallen at all," he said, and bent down to release the bindings before her hips split from the pressure. Digging into his pocket, he whipped out a rubber clamp and fastened her skis together. Then he stepped out of his own and did the same to those.

"What are you doing?" she asked suspiciously, the white boots with gold lightning on the sides finding tenuous purchase on the snow as he helped her up.

"Walking," he said. "You get the poles." Hefting a pair

of skis to each shoulder, he turned and headed toward the side of the slope.

Maggie scrambled after him, awkwardly clasping the poles in her gloved hands. "Told you this was the only way down."

He wasn't about to tell her they were only going to walk as far as the restaurant, which was just around the corner. Maybe on a full stomach, she'd be more amenable to giving it another try.

Then again, maybe not.

"You going to eat those?" Maggie pointed to the french fried potatoes on Will's plate.

He nodded and dug into his pocket. Tossing a couple of dollars across the table, he said, "Go get yourself some more, Maggie. These are mine."

She grinned. "You're not going to get them for me?"

"Uh-uh. I've already stood in that line twice. It's your turn."

She shrugged and awkwardly climbed out of the bench seat, her boots clanging heavily on the patio's iron-mesh floor. "You want anything else?" she asked politely, her mind already on what she would buy with the two bucks.

"I think I'll survive until dinner," he said mildly, and shook his head at her appetite. "Are you sure that's enough money?"

"Hope so."

The lunch lines had shortened considerably since they'd arrived at the open-air restaurant, and in no time she was back at the table.

"It's a good thing you showed up when you did," she said, chewing on a curly fried potato as she clambered back onto the bench across from Will. She dipped another into a swirl of ketchup and chewed with absorbed pleasure. "I guess keeping my lunch money with the map wasn't such a terrific idea."

She was pleased Will refrained from telling her just how stupid that had been. After all, she hadn't done it intentionally, but it still managed to look like another bubbleheaded stunt.

"I scratched my boots," she went on to confess, plopping a boot onto the bench and pointing to a jagged scar just below the lightning strike. "That guy in the rental shop is going to kill me."

"It's not a problem. I'll go with you when you return them just in case Scott throws a fit." Will watched entranced as she ran her fingers through her hair. It was nearly dry now, thanks to the warming rays that fell from a cloudless sky, and was turning golden as it dried, the white highlights sparkling in the sunshine. She was so effortlessly beautiful, he thought, and wondered why she'd layered on the cosmetics the evening before. She certainly didn't need them.

He wished he knew her well enough to tell her so. "Scott can fix that little mark on your boots so that they look like new." Well, almost new.

Maggie said thanks, and noticed that he was surprised by the breathless relief in her voice. She realized he thought she was nervous about the scratch, and she let him go on thinking it.

It wouldn't do to tell him that any excuse to be with him was sufficient to send her heart racing.

He asked her what she did for a living—in Vacaville, wasn't it?—and she mumbled something about working in an office, then changed the subject. Telling him that she was office manager for a large accounting firm would detract from Bambi Bubblehead's credibility, to say the least.

Besides, she planned on quitting in the near future to try something else. Anything else.

Finding the perfect job was the follow-up to this weekend's project—discovering her own sensuality. Not just a job, she corrected herself. A career. Something that would fulfill her sense of self-worth and be fun at the same time. Something she really wanted to do. She didn't have a clue what that elusive career might be—not a practical career, at any rate.

Will imagined she was a receptionist or the like, and

since she obviously didn't want to talk about it, he guessed that she wasn't happy in her job.

He wondered if there were any openings at the hotel.

Stuffing her mouth with more french fries, Maggie wished she had the nerve to ask Will what he was doing on the mountain. The night before, when she'd asked if there was any chance they'd run into each other on the slopes that day, he'd said he had to work.

She groaned, knowing now that it was pure luck they hadn't. Run into each other, that is. After all, she'd already managed to crash into an alarming number of people that day.

Still, it didn't make sense that he was there. She slid a glance across the table and found his blue-gray gaze fixed on her.

"I was annoyed to find you gone this morning," he said.

Maggie gulped. She'd known it was wrong to leave without saying something, wrong to slip out before he was even awake.

But she'd been too aware of her own shortcomings to stay. She was inexperienced in the intricacies of saying thank you and good-bye to a lover she knew she'd never meet again.

She hadn't wanted to say good-bye at all.

"I guess I assumed you wouldn't want a morning after," she said.

He stared at her for a long moment before speaking, his eyes glinting like cold steel in the afternoon sunshine. "You expected me to pick up my clothes and get out of your life," he said harshly.

Maggie was confused. "I thought that's what you wanted . . . one night."

"It was. I changed my mind."

Her heart leapt as his words sank in. *I changed my mind.* He wasn't the only one.

"What if I told you I'm not ready to let you go?" he asked softly.

She chewed nervously on her bottom lip. "I'd be . . . surprised. I didn't expect you to want anything more from me, now that we'd, well . . ." Embarrassed, she let her voice trail off and hid her flushed face behind her hands.

Will felt acute hatred for the man who had instilled such a complete lack of confidence in her, but restrained his anger for an appropriate target, such as the punching bag at the gym. Maggie hadn't done anything to deserve the anger.

"You mentioned last night that you have three days' vacation," he said.

"Yes." The answer was muffled, and he reached across the table to tug her hands from her face.

He caught her gaze with his own, holding her to a promise she couldn't even begin to understand. "Spend them with me."

He watched as surprise was overwhelmed by excitement. It sent shivers up his spine as he realized she was so damned appreciative of the little he had to give.

Someone needed to teach her to expect more. To demand it.

"Three days? With you?"

He nodded.

"That reeks of a relationship, Will," she teased, trying desperately to regain her equilibrium. She hadn't expected this, hadn't dared to hope.

Three days. It was an eternity.

"A short relationship, perhaps," he said.

"Some marriages don't last that long."

"Don't get any ideas about marriage," he said flatly. "I don't believe in it."

"But I thought truck drivers were the marrying kind," she said, forcing a light tone though she was stunned by his reprimand. It had only been a joke.

"I'm not a truck driver." Will sighed and realized she'd never think of him otherwise. "And I'm never going to marry. Not ever." He hoped that at least that point would sink in.

Never say never. Maggie flirted with the temptation to throw his own words back in his face, but elected to retreat in the face of his blatant lack of humor on the subject.

"Who's talking about marriage?" she asked, spreading her hands in a placating gesture. "I'm still back there where you asked me to spend my vacation with you . . . assuming the offer's still open."

He studied her for a long moment until he was satisfied the subject of marriage had been dropped. "The offer is there. Will you?" His heart beat erratically as he awaited the words that would give him so much pleasure.

Maggie nodded slowly, then ducked her head to stare at her lap in an all out effort to compose herself. He wanted her! A few days, that's all it was, she told herself. Don't get carried away.

And don't even joke about marriage! She would have laughed had she not been so overwhelmed by his request. No one had ever wanted her before. Not for herself. Not really.

She raised her head and said quite clearly, "Yes. I think I'd like that."

"It's done, then." Will looked away so she couldn't see how incredibly relieved he was. She'd said yes, and that was all that mattered. He absorbed the pleasure she'd just given him, the joy, then schooled his expression to something other than total relief before turning back to face her.

There was a tiny smile on her lips when she asked, "What if I'd said no?"

He grinned, afraid of nothing now that he had what he wanted. "It's a big mountain, Maggie, and I haven't gotten you off it yet."

"Threats, Will?" she asked, clearly seeing the determination in his gaze.

"Promises, Maggie love," he said. "And you owe me."

A morning after, he told himself. Time together. She owed him that much.

Then maybe he'd be able to put his fascination for her aside and get on with the rest of his life.

Five

It was late afternoon when they staggered through the French doors that led from the hotel's observation deck into the bar. Almost blinded by the change from sunshine to dusk, Will busied himself in brushing the snow from Maggie's shoulders, back, and behind. Then he shucked his boots and knelt down to help Maggie with hers.

By the time he straightened, his eyes had adjusted enough to see the look on her face. It was exhausted and happy and triumphant.

He felt that a small sign of gratitude would have been appropriate. After all, he'd saved her from Skiers' Hell.

Maggie just smiled at him and proceeded to empty her pockets of snow. With a snort of disgust, he grabbed a piece of her parka at about shoulder level and steered her away from the door.

"Find some powder, Maggie?" Biff asked as they padded in stocking feet to the bar.

"Here and there," she said vaguely, too tired to remember the powder pants routine she'd spun for him the night before. She was just grateful to be alive.

"Two whiskeys, up," Will told Biff, lifting Maggie onto a bar stool, then taking the one beside her.

"I don't like whiskey," Maggie said, spying a bowl of nuts. She snagged it with the only two fingers that weren't frozen stiff and started to eat.

"They're both for me," Will said. "Biff will get you a glass of wine in a minute. *After* he gets the whiskey." Skiers' Hell had taken its toll on him too.

"You sound like you've had a busy day out there, Boss," Biff said, making quick work of the drinks. He bypassed the nicety of bar napkins and plunked the drinks in front of Will. "I don't remember the last time you took a weekday off to ski."

"Boss?" Maggie said.

"White, pink, or red?" Biff asked.

Will groaned. "She likes white," he said, lifting one shot glass. He was in the mood to punch out the man behind the bar, who was a cousin by birth and a friend by accident. Biff—Barley Irwin Fuller to those in the know—was working in the bar because he'd spent most of his "allowance" for the year on a horse that had finished last at Hialeah, then landed on Will's doorstep. The executor of his trust fund wasn't speaking to him. His parents—aunt and uncle to Will and currently somewhere in the Seychelles having a blast, naturally— were apparently unconcerned that their charming but seemingly directionless son had been reduced to earning his room and board via menial labor.

Will hadn't had a choice. Family was family. He'd hired Biff with reservations and the sure knowledge that by the time Biff reached his thirty-fourth birthday—thus "earning" yet another year's allotment out of the millions he was slated to come into when he turned thirty-five—he'd surely take off for a cozier environment.

He hadn't, though. He'd stayed and become Will's friend. And Casey's. And Will had seen three or four children nipping at Biff's heels once in a while, but hadn't pressed the younger man for an explanation.

Biff hadn't offered one.

Just as he hadn't explained why he'd been so handy when a couple of undisciplined thugs from a casino down the hill had decided to have yet another try at convincing Will that he wanted to sell out. In the past, Will had been able to sidestep the "friendly" persuasion that occurred with semiannual precision. That night, he hadn't. Unbeknownst to their fairly civilized boss, who'd only threatened but never followed through, they'd come looking for a fight. Will had resigned himself to giving them one when, unexpectedly, a shadow had joined the fray.

Biff, pretty much without Will's assistance, had convinced the thugs never to try again.

He'd dispatched the bad guys in a series of moves that were decidedly foreign and not recognizable to a man who hadn't studied the martial arts. Will had, and he'd recognized Biff's expertise with the respect a student gives a master.

Biff was a friend. He was family. He was also a bit of a mystery.

Will thought he might strangle him any moment now.

"Biff, why did you call him Boss?" Maggie asked, watching out of the corner of her eye as Will downed the whiskey in one gulp. It was the bartender, though, who had her full attention. She studied him carefully, her gaze skimming over the harshly drawn lines of his face, the nearly black eyes staring back at her from beneath equally dark brows. There were secrets in those eyes, she realized, the least of which was probably the subject at hand.

Will slammed the empty shot glass down on the bar and coughed, catching the brief flicker of surprise in Biff's expression before it was replaced with curious amusement.

Biff handed him a glass of water without taking his gaze off Maggie. "Boss is something I call a lot of people around here," he said easily.

"That's mostly because just about everyone here outranks you," Will said dryly, and sipped the second whiskey with more caution than before. He'd needed the first one.

It had taken three and a half hours to coax Maggie

down the mountain. The ski patrol had been no help whatsoever, unless you called warning other late-afternoon skiers of the peril heading toward them "help." Will had actually considered leaving Maggie for the ski patrol to deal with . . . but then he'd remembered the Old Geezers' Slalom Race and the arrangements he'd already coordinated with the patrol.

His conscience almost bothered him when he recalled the temptation, though. His patience had been sorely tried that afternoon.

"So why'd Biff call you Boss?" Maggie asked, ignoring the wine and stealing a sip of water from Will's glass. "Is that your nickname?" It was so damned hard, she thought, being this close to Will and having to remember that her bubblehead persona was part and parcel of what he expected to see.

She was so tired of pretending to be so dense that she could hardly think.

Will glared at Biff. "I bought this place a couple years ago," he finally said.

Will owned the resort? Was this what he'd meant the night before when he'd said he worked in real estate? She almost laughed at the understatement, but refrained. The man who had helped a certain bubblehead off the mountain that day obviously hadn't wanted her to know that he was as wealthy as he was nice.

It almost irked her to think Will believed Bambi Bubblehead could possibly have any financially predatory instincts.

Still, she decided to let him keep his little secret. "You own the bar?" she asked, wide-eyed and unquestionably impressed. "Gee, I didn't know you could own just one room of a building. Is this kind of like a condominium, but you don't get a bedroom?"

It was almost impossible for her to ignore Biff, who was so obviously laughing behind clenched teeth. She couldn't afford to notice, though, because then her own laughter wouldn't be far behind. Reprieve came when Biff avoided looking at either her or Will as he busily polished the bar.

"No, Maggie—"

She interrupted before Will had a chance to explain. She didn't want him to explain. Whether he owned this room or the entire resort wasn't important. it was, however, terrific fodder for her alter ego.

"Did you consider buying the disco at the other end of the building?" she asked seriously. "Because it seems to me that they get a lot more business than this place." She glanced around the half-empty room, biting her lip against the pressing need to laugh at the incredulous expression on Will's face.

"Somebody else probably already bought the good parts before you could get to them," she went on, then ate another handful of nuts as she gave it serious consideration. "I'll bet the people who own the dining room make a mint."

Will shut his eyes and sighed, giving up any inclination to set her straight. It just wasn't worth the trouble. Opening his eyes, he saw Biff was almost choking from his efforts not to laugh.

"I can't imagine anyone wanting to buy the reception desk," she said with a giggle. "I mean, what would you say if someone asked you what you did for a living? 'I own a reception desk.'" She shook her head. "That sounds about as interesting as stuffing envelopes."

Swallowing over his own threatening chuckles, he asked Biff if he would call the kitchen and see if they had something handy in the way of hot hors d'oeuvres because Maggie was hungry.

The bowl of nuts was empty.

"How does the guy who owns the restrooms make any money?" she asked as Biff turned to pick up the telephone.

Will finally got his morning after. It followed their second night together, and it ended with breakfast.

Maggie asked for eggs, bacon, and hash browns, then added a side of French toast to the order before the waiter left the private dining alcove Will had managed to secure for them.

He merely raised his eyebrows and said, "You have the appetite of a truck driver."

"How would you know?" she asked. "I thought you said you weren't a truck—"

"Don't start that again, Maggie," he said firmly. "It's too early and I haven't had enough sleep to keep up with you."

Maggie smiled indulgently, reaching across the table to touch him lightly on the back of his hand. Any excuse, she told herself. "I *know* you told me you were in real estate, but it seems to me a fancy way of saying you own a bar."

Again, he ignored the urge to set her straight. Her fingers captured his attention, her touch an electrifying reminder of the night they'd spent in each other's arms. Making love with Maggie was so extraordinarily exciting that even now it set his heart thudding. Even now, sitting across the table from her, not yet an hour since he'd thrust himself into her honeyed warmth, he felt the blood rush through his veins with a heated urgency that made an hour ago seem like years.

He wanted her again.

Maggie watched his eyes cloud with passion, and was filled with a heady sensation of satisfaction that eclipsed forever the ghosts of her past. Will wanted her, needed her in a way she'd never been needed before.

It unnerved her to admit she needed him too. Needed, but couldn't have. Not for any reason. He'd made his position clear. And she'd made up her mind to savor every minute of the day—and night—that was left.

She settled back in her chair and let him sizzle, her own eyes dancing with mischief as she watched him over her second cup of coffee.

The first had been served amid rumpled sheets and bunched pillows. She didn't know whether it was the discreet knock at the door, the aroma of fresh-brewed coffee, or the almost painful brightness of the day as Will pulled open the drapes that had jolted her from sleep. All three, she'd rather suspected as she'd tugged at the sheets, struggling to erect a facade of composure and modesty amidst the telltale signs of their lovemaking.

He hadn't seemed to notice her discomfiture as he handed her a cup of coffee, kissed her on the forehead, and asked her if she'd join him for breakfast in the dining room after she dressed.

"Please," he added when she hesitated.

She said that of course she'd dress and acted offended that he needed to remind her. The giggles had been almost impossible to suppress, especially when she caught the dismayed look on his face—the look that meant he wanted to explain himself but was beginning to realize it wasn't worth the trouble.

He left mere seconds before she lost the battle. Doubling over in a fit of laughter that eventually made her sides ache and her coffee spill onto the sheets, she savored the moment and knew she'd never forget his expression for as long as she lived.

She wished he could share in the joke.

Will refilled their cups and settled back against the leather cushions of his chair. She was so incredibly beautiful, her face fresh and clear, devoid of all makeup but for a touch of mascara and blush. Over dinner the night before, he'd finally gotten up the nerve to tell her how gorgeous she was without the heavy cosmetics she'd used that first night. When she started laughing in the middle of his "you've got beautiful skin" lecture, he'd been puzzled.

"Go figure," she'd said obscurely, and he'd been left wondering what the joke was.

Not that it mattered. There wasn't much that made a great deal of sense with Maggie.

He sipped his coffee in total contentment and knew that he didn't care. There was so much about her that was perfectly . . . perfect.

Waking up to Maggie, sharing the morning hours with her . . . Such a luxury, he thought, and knew that he'd never felt so pampered in his life. The only thing better would be to touch her, to caress her as he'd done last night . . . to submit as she caressed him.

Feeling emotional and wonderfully aroused by his heated gaze, Maggie elected to inject a dose of bubble-head into the conversation—just in case either of them had forgotten who she really was. "How do you ever manage to sell houses if you're constantly pretending to be a truck driver?" she asked with a note of bewilderment.

"I've never pretended to be a truck driver," he said in a low growl. "And if you know what's good for you, you'll drop that."

She shrugged. "You're the one who brought it up."

"I was merely commenting on your appetite."

"Then you should have said I eat like a horse," she said matter-of-factly. "Everyone knows what that means."

He nodded. "I guess I thought comparing you to a horse wasn't flattering."

"I *like* horses," she said, as though astonished to discover he might not.

"So do I," he said quickly. "Next time I won't be afraid to compare you to one." He couldn't believe it when she looked pleased.

"You think being compared to a truck driver should make me feel terrific?" she asked, right in the middle of his sigh of relief.

Will knew he had only one chance to end this one. "You're too beautiful to be a truck driver."

She grinned, then leaned forward so no one else could hear. "I think you're beautiful too," she confided, "but you won't be if a truck driver hears you saying things like that. After all, there are lots of lady truck drivers who I'm sure are perfectly lovely to look at."

Will groaned.

"The men aren't too bad either."

He groaned again.

"You know, Will, if a truck driver comes into the bar—speaking of which, I really think you should have a real office—anyway, if a truck driver comes along and he's looking for a house, I'd advise you to let someone else handle it. It'll be much safer." She leaned back as the waiter returned with the three laden plates that consisted of her breakfast and a bowl of oat bran for Will.

"I'll remember your advice the next time a truck driver comes in," he said gravely, not for a moment considering telling her that he didn't sell houses at all.

He drank coffee and watched as she took an eager bite of eggs and potatoes. Must be metabolism, he mused. Or maybe thinking like she did took a lot of energy. Either way, Maggie certainly didn't have to watch what she ate. Halfway wishing he was afflicted with the screwy thought processes of the woman across the table, he added skim milk to his hot cereal and began to eat.

Suddenly, she dropped her fork and stared across the table at him. Her expression was stunned as she said in a small voice, "No one's ever told me that before."

"That they'll take your advice?" He could believe that one.

She shook her head. "No. No one has ever told me that I'm beautiful."

Impossible! he thought. But then he remembered. Only two days ago he'd considered her to be merely pretty. How wrong he'd been. Maggie glowed with such beauty, she took his breath away.

"Of course you're beautiful, Maggie," he said. Seeing her eyes soften, he knew he'd reached her somewhere close to her heart. "Cheryl wouldn't have been so furious if you weren't beautiful."

"Cheryl?" she asked, bewildered . . . and hurt for a reason she didn't dare examine.

"The woman I was avoiding that first night." He'd hurt her, made a mistake that had wounded. He should never have mentioned Cheryl. The sick feeling in his stomach was less punishment than he deserved.

Had Maggie been more sophisticated, she would have

been flattered. But she wasn't and he knew that now. Maggie was neither sophisticated nor flattered.

He had to admire her for both.

"Of course," she said. "Cheryl."

Will couldn't help but try to make amends. She looked so pained, so alone.

He hated that.

"I can't believe I'm the first man to tell how beautiful you are," he said, dropping the Cheryl mistake like the bomb it was and reaffirming the basic truth with which he'd begun.

"You are," Maggie whispered. The pain was less now. Not because of his flattery, but because he'd realized how she'd reacted to his words and cared enough to remedy it.

He was a good man.

Will watched, mesmerized and relieved as her lips curved into a smile that gave a whole new meaning to beauty. He was pleased by her response, touched that such simple, honest words gave her so much pleasure. But she wasn't supposed to look at him as though she was half in love with him.

"Don't look at me like that," he warned with a mock-serious expression that was half teasing, half reprimanding. He *had* to do it, get that half-in-love look out of her eyes before she got hurt very badly indeed.

"Like what?"

"Like you're falling in love," he said, leaning across the table to speak quietly in the suddenly still alcove. "If you're not careful, I'll think you're letting your emotions run wild."

It had been a gentle lesson, he hoped.

Her brows lifted in delicate affront. "As if I would," she said softly.

He eased back in his chair, sipped his coffee, and wondered why he didn't feel perfectly contented with the world.

Maggie forced a little smile to accompany her next words. "Besides, Will, I promised my mother I'd never fall for a truck driver."

He glared at her, and she knew she'd succeeded in diverting him. Taking a measured breath, she lowered her gaze and studied the table between them.

Silly to be upset, she told herself. Unnecessary. Pushing aside the empty egg plate, she positioned the French toast in its place and began to coat the golden slices liberally with hot syrup. Then she dug into the treat as though she hadn't already made it through a full plate of breakfast.

Distress rarely interfered with her appetite. Neither did it fade as she ate. She was getting in too deep, she told herself. Three days, he'd promised her, and here she was, hanging on to his every word . . . imagining the two of them together for much longer than the three days they'd agreed to. Her emotions *were* running wild, finding seed in her heart and instantly springing into full bloom.

She could almost imagine she was falling in love.

Maggie all but licked her plate, so intent were her thoughts. She had to leave, she decided. Now, not tomorrow.

Before it was too late.

Before he discovered he'd been right.

She composed her expression, then lifted her gaze to meet his. He'd been watching her, she realized, probably wondering if she was going to get all possessive and such.

She had a surprise for him.

"Did I ever mention why I came to Tahoe?" she asked.

He smiled. "It wasn't for the skiing, I gather."

She shook her head and blurted out the truth in a manner that was designed to shock. "It was sex," she said succinctly. "My ex-husband left me with a lot of hang-ups and I finally decided to see if I could get rid of them."

"Sex?" he murmured, less surprised by her admission than he was by her tone of voice. He'd expected something like this from the beginning—she'd been almost transparent in her inexperience. He'd watched for two nights now, satisfied and incredibly stimulated, as she learned from each sensual adventure and then asked for more.

His body hardened as he remembered her sexy voice when she'd whispered into his ear the things she wanted to do again—and why.

But now, she sounded as though she wanted to put him in his place.

She nodded energetically. "You see, that's why I was so worried when you said you hadn't done this before. I needed feedback, and for a minute there you almost had me believing you had more problems than I did! You see, I only had three days' vacation to get it sorted out."

"Sex isn't something you could, er, *sort out* in Vacaville?" he asked, wondering how long he could stand it before he dragged her back to her room to resume where they'd left off.

"No. Besides the fact I didn't want to risk having a humiliating experience with someone I might bump into in the grocery store one day, I didn't want to take the chance that he might want more than a fling."

"You're afraid of a relationship?"

"Not afraid," she said firmly. "I just don't want one. I like my life like it is, just me depending on me." It was safer that way.

Will's flash of anger was partially subdued by a burning, uncontrollable fear. He wanted to shake some sense into her for putting herself into such a potentially dangerous position with her sexual experiment. No telling what could have happened if she'd tried this with another man with fewer scruples, a man who might object to being used in the way she described. A man who might take advantage of her in ways she couldn't even begin to imagine.

She might have been hurt. Or worse.

Maggie gritted her teeth behind her enthusiastic smile, seeing the anger that crossed his expression before he got it under control. She wondered at that, the anger.

She'd thought he would be pleased.

"I was relieved when you said you weren't in the market for a relationship," she said as further support for her explanation. "That would have been a mess, what with you living so far away and me not wanting one in the first place."

Will shuttered his gaze from hers, considering for a moment the impulse to drag her back up to Skiers' Hell and frighten her so much that she'd never lie to him again.

Because he knew she was lying.

He ignored the accessory details and went back to the crux of the matter. "Have I provided you with adequate feedback, Maggie?"

She swallowed hard, wishing she had been just a little less bold and a lot more cautious in her approach. Too late. He was furious and the full impact of it was centered on her.

"Absolutely," she whispered, then got a grip on her roiling emotions. "Sex isn't something I'll ever have doubts about. Not ever."

"And that's all we have in common, isn't it, Maggie . . . sex?"

She nodded, knowing it was the answer he wanted.

Her response—even though he'd expected it—was as painful as it was annoying. There was more between them than sex. He'd wager his soul on it. But, for some reason, Maggie didn't want to admit it, and damned if he was going to beg.

It didn't occur to him that the things he wanted her to admit were exactly what he'd discouraged her from anticipating just five minutes earlier.

One corner of his mouth lifted in a sardonic grin. "You're right, Maggie love. A person would have to be snow-blind to imagine anything else."

She smiled through the shaft of pain that ripped open her heart. "Of course. Snow-blind. Isn't that what happened to Hercules when he crossed the Andes?"

His answering smile was almost genuine. "Hannibal," he said gently. "And it was the Alps."

"Him too?"

He nodded without venturing to correct her.

She shrugged. "Well, a mountain's a mountain whichever way you look at it, and my little car likes to take its sweet time going up them *and* down. Those curves are murder if you're not careful." She took a final sip of coffee, then pushed back her chair and stood up.

"Where are you going?" he asked, moving quickly to block her path.

"Vacaville," she said brightly. "Didn't I mention I'd decided to leave today?"

Six

He'd never got a chance to tell Maggie he loved her.

Will slouched in the leather seat of his truck and watched the single-story home across the road, waiting for Maggie to come home. He'd pulled her address from the hotel files, totally ignoring Casey's mild admonition that perhaps she wasn't interested in seeing him again. Why else hadn't she given him the information herself?

Because he'd hurt her. First he'd made that crack about Cheryl, then he'd half accused her of falling in love—like it was a crime or something! And if that wasn't enough, there was that *stupid* line about being snow-blind! Will took a deep breath and understood now how it was that wars started. Things were said in self-defense, lies really, but they hurt just the same.

A relationship with Maggie was something he wanted more than just about anything he could imagine. And certainly more than the three days she'd promised, the two they'd had. Screw the distance, her ditziness . . . his stupidity. He could make it work, be with her as long as it took to get over the way she made him feel. Stay with her until the love he felt for her wore out and finally disappeared. Will wasn't crazy enough to imagine it would last forever. It never did.

Not that he'd personally, *actually* been in love before. But he had a mountain of experience with friends who'd married for love and divorced amidst a tumult of hate. His own parents had shown him that love never lasted.

He was convinced that the only marriages that survived were those practical relationships in which the two participants had too much in common to worry about the emotional deterioration over the years.

Casey had tried to convince him otherwise, but Will wasn't buying it. After all, Casey and Harriet had been married a paltry two years. Even if Will considered Harriet the perfect companion for his friend, he knew deep down that it would never last. Not the love and certainly not the passion.

It wasn't going to happen to him.

It had taken him a week to come to her, seven days of trying to put her from his mind, seven nights of dying a little each time that he reached for her and found her missing.

Seven nights of remembering just how good it had been between them.

> "I've never ever done this before," he said, panting hard as he toiled to match the hard pace she set, then gritting his teeth when it seemed as though she was going to leave him by the wayside in a breathless heap.
>
> She glanced over her shoulder and grinned. "Me, neither. And from all accounts, I'd say I was a natural."
>
> He grabbed her by the hips and brought their bodies solidly together. Holding tight, he murmured into her ear other things she was naturally good at.
>
> Ice skating, it seemed, was just one more.
>
> She'd insisted upon giving skating a try, even though she should have been exhausted from her day on Skiers' Hell. She was tired, she

admitted, but it seemed a shame not to try it once.

Just an hour or so, she pleaded with her very best smile, to fill the time before dinner.

Even though he had better ideas for that hour, he agreed. He'd agree to anything when she flashed that incredible smile at him.

They fell, of course. Not even a gifted amateur could be expected to maintain her balance against such blatantly suggestive nonsense.

Which wasn't really nonsense at all.

Dinner with Maggie had been just another taste of ecstasy. Temptation and desire warred with restraint as they laughed and teased and, sometimes, even talked about mundane things . . . things like what prize he should put up for the Old Geezers' Slalom Race the following week.

She'd suggested a balaclava to hide the old guy's gray hair and he pretended affront, reminding her that he too, would participate in the race . . . although it was his first year.

She giggled and told him that while a sweater would hide his three little gray hairs from the world, she'd always know better. . . .

Will awoke to the first rays of morning, incredibly content to find Maggie sprawled beside him, her hair sticking out every which way and soft snores coming from her mouth. In the drawer beside the bed, he found the last packet of protection he'd bought the night before to supplement Maggie's dwindling stock. When he was ready, he turned to her, slowly, insistently awakening her with his touch.

Making love with Maggie was as good as it could get. Playing with her, sharing the hours outside of bed as much as in. . . . He'd never before experienced such total contentment.

He was in love.

It wouldn't last. He knew that, but it didn't matter. Maggie was all that counted now.

Their relationship would be fun and lively and exciting. Maggie might be a bit disconnected with the rest of the world, but he didn't care. As long as she agreed to be with him, she could be whatever kind of person she wished and he wouldn't stand in her way.

She made him feel something he'd never felt before, and that made her more important to him than any other woman he'd ever known.

He stared out through the windshield that was speckled with the final drops of that evening's rain storm. It was past eight o'clock, long past the time when he'd thought she would have been at home. After all, how late did a receptionist have to work?

Unless she had a date.

He rolled down the window and drummed his fingers on the side of the truck. He sincerely hoped she wouldn't be too difficult about accepting his apology. He hadn't meant to hurt her. Still, he wasn't yet sure what he was going to say that would make her understand that the rules hadn't changed.

An orange Volkswagen chugged down the street and pulled into her driveway. She was home. He breathed a sigh of relief. *Finally!* He rolled up the window just in case it rained again during the night.

He didn't have to be back in Tahoe until noon the next day.

He was reaching for his jacket when he saw a man crawl out of the passenger side of the orange car. He was dressed in a green flight suit of the sort worn by military pilots, but Will was too far away to distinguish rank or anything else.

He stiffened as he watched Maggie skirt the car's hood to where the blond man was waiting, rubbing his back, obviously exaggerating a complaint about the confines of the small car.

She laughed and reached into the backseat. Pulling out a smallish green bag, she tossed it at the man. He shoved it back into her arms, dropping a kiss on her forehead before leaning back into the car and reappearing with two more bags. Large ones.

One appeared to be an oversized briefcase, black and battered. The other was green and looked like some sort of suitcase.

The blond man hefted the two larger bags and followed Maggie into the house.

Will waited until the door closed behind them before starting his vehicle. Hooking the gears into first, he drove slowly down the street.

Maggie, it seemed, had enough complications in her life.

She didn't need another.

Dawn was just around the corner, elusive but imminent all the same.

Matt flicked back the curtains and looked out at the street. "My ride's here, Maggie," he said, thrusting his arms into a heavy green flight jacket. "See you next time around."

Maggie yawned and waved with the hand that wasn't covering her mouth. She didn't have the energy for anything else.

Matt grinned and opened the front door. Hefting all three bags, he blew a kiss toward the woman in the chair beside the fireplace then left, kicking the door shut behind him.

"Thank God," Maggie breathed, too tired even to consider walking back to her bed.

She didn't feel badly about not walking Matt to the door. It had been enough of a gesture that she'd awakened when she'd heard the phone alert just thirty minutes earlier. Fixing Matt a hot breakfast while he showered was simply a measure of sisterly affection that didn't extend to overt perkiness at o-four-awful in the morning.

Being related to an air force pilot sometimes meant that life happened at weird positions of the clock, and Maggie had never accustomed herself to it. There hadn't been much of an excuse for getting used to the odd hours, since Matt was stationed clear on the other side of the country and landed with irregular frequency at Travis Air Force Base—just a few minutes' drive from Vacaville.

Her only brother had been pleased that at least she was home this time. His last pass through had been a week ago—about the time she was making a fool of herself at Lake Tahoe. Maggie shuddered, her toes curling beneath her thickly quilted robe as she remembered the total airhead she'd played.

Will probably didn't even remember her name.

It had been such a temptation to stay for another night . . . for a lifetime.

That hadn't been one of the choices. Will had made his feelings on permanency clear. Relationships were okay as long as they were terminal in nature. He didn't believe in marriage.

She wasn't even sure he believed in love.

Maggie rocked back in the chair, wondering if she believed in it herself. Certainly, she'd thought herself in love with her husband. That had fallen apart, though, and the only thing she felt now was regret that she'd even considered spending her entire life with such a sleaze.

She had feelings for Will that went beyond anything she'd ever felt for anyone. Whether or not it was love, she'd never know.

She smiled—something that happened fairly often these days—and knew she had something that no one could ever take away. She had a memory.

It was a fine one as memories go . . . of a man who had shown her that life was wonderful and exciting.

She had her journal too.

Its pages gave her comfort as well as providing an outlet for emotions that were as bittersweet as they were disturbingly exciting. She clung to them as her only link with the affair that was over and done with. But there was something new about her writing, something quite surprising.

There was a depth and clarity that penetrated her journal and crossed over to her stories, until she knew she was writing at a new level. Everything she wrote was suddenly more real than before, more mature. When the words flowed from her heart and onto the paper, she felt the muted thunder of excitement.

She wished she could have shared this with Will, not as a dream but as a hobby of sorts. That way, she wouldn't have to tell him her fantasies of becoming a writer yet could still share the stories that were part of her soul, her life.

Will wasn't there to share anything with, though. She missed him.

Sighing, Maggie pushed herself up from the chair and trailed down the hall to her bedroom. She had a big day tomorrow, a meeting with the boss to pitch her anticipated requirements for office personnel if the proposed expansion took place. She wished she could get more excited about it, but she couldn't, and that was why she was getting her résumé in order. It was time to move on.

Would she ever find her dream career? Would it be as satisfying as the nights she'd spent in Will's arms?

Not surprisingly, she was still smiling as she climbed beneath the covers. She almost always ended up smiling when she thought about Will.

And miss him or not, it was over.

Life went on.

Somehow.

Seven

It took him by surprise, like a punch in the gut when all you were expecting was a slap on the face. Will switched off the telephone's loudspeaker and lifted the receiver to his ear. The words Maggie had said were still vibrating in the explosive quiet of his office, and he couldn't stand to hear them like that again!

"Say that again," he demanded, listening hard now because he wanted to know *precisely* what she was feeling and he couldn't do that very well over the phone. But it was all he had at the moment, so he just had to try.

"I said I had a miscarriage. I thought you'd want to know."

He'd been wrong. Changing the method of delivery hadn't made the words any less abrasive. He gripped the receiver hard and didn't say anything. He couldn't. The pain was too raw.

He knew there were things he had to ask her, things he had to learn, because until now he hadn't even known about the life she'd carried within her, the child they'd evidently created in a moment of passion so intense, he'd had to try to force the entire episode from his mind. He really hadn't believed he'd see her again, not when she'd seemed so happy in another man's company.

That had been four months before. After all, there was nothing between them that he hadn't had with other women, was there? She was just a ditzy blonde he'd taken a liking to because . . . well, because he kind of liked her. The circular argument was typical of how he thought about Maggie, and considering how often he'd thought of her in the last four months, he was beginning to get comfortable with the pattern. Maggie was a revolving door when it came to contradictions and logic.

At least, he thought her name was Maggie.

Considering the way they'd met, he wouldn't be surprised if she'd borrowed a name to go along with the fantasy she'd engineered. But somehow, Margaret Ann Cooper—*Mac to my friends but you can call me Maggie*—didn't sound like an alias designed to go along with seduction.

It never occurred to him to question her basic assumption that he was, in fact, the father. Maggie wouldn't lie about something as intimate as that. He couldn't explain how he knew, but dammit, there were some things a man just knew about the woman with whom he'd shared so much . . . and so little.

As for the man he'd seen with her that night in Vacaville, Will dismissed him completely. Maggie apparently had.

"Maggie? Are you still there?" He was listening hard and he couldn't hear anything at all, no breathing, nothing.

"I'm here." Maggie covered the mouthpiece again with her hand. It was hard enough to get the words out much less suppress altogether the intermittent sniffle or sob. The last thing she wanted was for him to know how hard she was taking it.

He deserved to know about the miscarriage. She'd realized that after twelve hours of intense debate with herself, a debate that had been a blessing in disguise.

Trying to decide whether or not to tell him had some- how eased the heartache of that morning's loss, if only for a few brief moments.

Any relief was welcome. She'd never *ever* felt so completely alone in her life, not even when her parents had died in that stupid helicopter crash in Saudi Arabia. She'd had her brother to share her grief then, and it had somehow been easier to accept than this senseless accident of fate. Her parents had been older, they had lived . . . and loved.

Her baby hadn't even taken its first breath.

"Maggie?" Will said again. He sensed that she was waiting for him to push her into the details, giving him the choice, as though she imagined he might not want to know.

He had to know. "When?"

She'd done the right thing. A wave of relief washed over her as she gave thanks that he really was the man she remembered and not some inflated fantasy she'd created in her mind to make what she'd done seem more palatable. Instinct had told her Will would want to know. And he hadn't questioned his parentage of the baby. He'd known it was his.

She took a deep breath before lifting her hand from the mouthpiece. "This morning, early," she said, then rushed to give him the rest of it before the terrible pressure in her chest stopped her from speaking. "I was getting ready for work, and I was in a hurry because I'd promised Helen I'd pick up the cake for Ed's promotion party on the way to the office and I guess I must have slipped or something." He'd understand that, she knew. Her lack of coordination hadn't been part of the act. It was just there, an inescapable yet fortuitous complement to the alter ego she'd created.

"You fell?" he asked, anything to keep her talking. The words were so much better than the silences.

"Yes." She swallowed back the tears that were threat- ening because she had the worst part to go before she could hang up the telephone. "I was in the bathroom, and my feet went out from under me and I fell across the bathtub. When I tried to get up, I knew something was wrong. I got to the phone and called the paramedics, but it was too late when they got there."

Too late! She covered the mouthpiece again. The tears had begun to fall and there wasn't anything she could do to stop them. He couldn't see her, she reminded herself, and maybe if she could let the tears roll she could release some of the pain and he wouldn't hear it.

It was important that he not know how totally devastated she was by all this. Would the bubblehead she'd portrayed in that hotel in Tahoe be in similar agony? She didn't know, and now there wasn't time to work it out. She should have thought about that before calling, she knew, but once the decision had been made she'd had to get it over with, quick, before she lost her nerve and went with Option II, notification by letter, no return address.

"What does the doctor say?" he asked.

"He said there wasn't anything anyone could have done, even if there had been someone to help, because it was already too late. A bad fall like that doesn't always result in a miscarriage, and he couldn't say why it happened to me. I guess my karma was on a down cycle."

"I don't mean about the miscarriage!" Will shouted, stopping himself too late from letting the anger show. She didn't need to deal with that, not now, not when there was nothing she could do about it. It wasn't her fault she couldn't always follow his train of thought. "I meant you. Are you all right now?"

"Yes." She threw a soggy tissue on the floor and grabbed another. The tears were getting everything wet and the phone was slippery with them. "He said I'll be fine—that I'm okay now. It was just an accident that didn't really hurt anything." Except the baby, but she just had to accept that and go on.

She couldn't let it destroy her. That's what the doctor had told her.

Will asked her where she was.

"In the hospital, but just until morning." The long

night loomed ahead, and she dreaded the silence it would bring, the stark feeling of being alone without the comfort of a baby growing within her.

"Is there anyone who can help you?" Her parents, she'd told him once, were dead. The only family she'd ever mentioned was a brother. He'd envied her her brother, because she'd spoken of him with a warmth he'd always associated with close family ties—something he'd never experienced.

"There's scads of people who could help," she said, "and my brother is en route from somewhere in the Pacific—Iceland, I think." It wasn't hard to return to character, she found. It was almost too easy.

Will didn't stop to tell her that her geography was slightly off kilter. He had a sudden thought. "Is your brother in the service?"

"Air force," she mumbled. "He's a pilot."

Four months wasted. He'd kick himself later, he decided. There was certainly plenty of reason for it.

"I can be there in a couple of hours," he said, reaching across his desk for the phone number of the pilot he used when he didn't want to fly the company plane by himself.

Maggie clutched the receiver to her heart and wished she could say yes, come. Maybe with him holding her in his arms she'd be able to get through this thing. Racking sobs shook her body as she fought against giving in to the luxury of being weak. She knew she couldn't say yes, not and save her sanity.

Saying good-bye to Will that first time had been hard enough. Twice was more than she could do, especially now, with her heart already breaking from the loss of a child she'd carried four whole months. With a determination that came from some inner source she'd never had to tap, she suppressed her cries of grief and lifted the receiver to her mouth.

"No, don't come. I'm going away for a couple of days, to a friend's place at the beach, before going back to work. My brother said he'd come out there and get some sun when he gets back, although it's a mystery to me how anyone can come home from the Pacific and want to work on a tan, especially in Northern California. And besides, there's really nothing you could do." She tried to put more backbone into it. "Thanks, though. It's kind of you to offer."

Will almost threw the phone against the wall. *Thanks, though? It's kind of you to offer?* Who did she think he was, a passing acquaintance she'd met at a tea party? He was the father of the child she'd just lost and *dammit* she wasn't going to shut him out!

He let her think he'd do it her way, though. No sense making her worry about what time he'd walk through the door. "You'll call me if you need anything?" he asked as he wondered how long it would take to find out which hospital she was in and just how difficult it would be to sneak past the nurses at that time of night.

She told him yes and was saying good-bye when he interrupted. There was something he had to say, if only to get it out into the open . . . for both of them. "Would you have told me about the baby if it had lived?"

For Maggie, answering that was almost as hard as telling him about the miscarriage. She didn't know the answer and couldn't promise she would have done the right thing. "I don't know," she said. "I like to think I would have, but I honestly don't know."

"I know you would have told me," he said quietly. "Sooner or later, you would have called."

"Thank you," she whispered, pressing the phone to her mouth. Her trembling was making it so hard to hold the instrument, but she didn't want to put it down, not yet. She gripped the metal bar on the hospital bed and pulled herself a little more upright.

"Was that the only reason you told me," he asked, "because you thought I should know?" He wanted her to tell him no, that she wanted so much more, that the nights and days they'd shared had left her feeling empty without him. Just as they'd left him, although he couldn't figure out why, because she was just another woman, no one special, not really.

"No," Maggie said. The tears returned, because her

thoughts suddenly returned to the baby that she'd never hold, thanks to a *stupid* accident that had killed the life growing within her. "I guess I didn't want her to pass through this world with only one person caring."

Her. It had been a girl. Will forced himself to listen to Maggie say good-bye, mumbled something that passed for the same, and put down the receiver. He hadn't had the nerve to ask before, hadn't wanted to inflict more pain by forcing her to define the child she'd lost in terms of male or female.

A girl. Somehow, knowing that made it worse.

Maggie heard the click and knew he was gone. She didn't move to hang up her phone, because she simply didn't have the energy. She was drained, emotionally exhausted to the point where even simple thoughts lay disconnected in her head, nothing making any sense at all. She fell back against the raised bed and lay there for the longest time, an hour or perhaps just a moment— time was irrelevant—her eyes closed to the sterile indifference of the hospital room.

It wasn't that nobody had cared, she thought, lifting her hand to see the telephone receiver inside her grasp and wondering what to do with it. As if it mattered, she mused, knowing nothing really mattered, not anymore. The hospital staff had been concerned, helpful, optimistic.

"It's not as bad as carrying it full term and then losing it," one nurse had said.

Wanna bet? Maggie had thought.

"You'll have another," the doctor had pronounced after checking her over and confirming that nothing had been irreparably damaged.

How can I have another . . . if I never see him again?

I know you would have told me, he'd said. *Sooner or later, you would have called.*

How could he be so bloody sure?

Maggie bent double to reach the table she'd shoved to the end of the bed, a flexible tray that held the telephone and flowers and get-well cards and—Why were people bringing her get-well cards? She wasn't sick!

She wasn't even pregnant.

Slamming the phone down in its cradle, she tried very hard to stay mad because that seemed to be her best defense. The only other emotion she'd feel if she let go of the anger was grief.

She'd felt an intense love for the baby she'd carried in her womb. From the moment she'd discovered she was pregnant, she had done everything possible to ensure it was born healthy.

A slip of the foot, a little fall . . . and her heart was breaking.

If only she'd never met Will, this wouldn't have happened. If only she'd never loved him.

Because she did love him. She'd stopped running from that fact months ago.

Her only problem was not knowing whether she loved the man who had so passionately invaded her senses . . . or the father of the child they'd created.

That it didn't matter was perfectly clear. She would never see Will again.

She would never know.

Eight

Maggie could have sworn she smelled food.

That was an overdose of wishful thinking, of course, because it was after ten o'clock and she'd been served her ration of stuffed peppers, mashed potatoes, and vanilla pudding along with the rest of the hospital detainees at least five hours earlier. She'd amazed the nurse by scarfing down everything on her tray—although she really only enjoyed the pudding. The nurse had been positively beaming when she saw the clean plates, saying something about how the return of one's appetite was the first sign of healing.

Maggie didn't bother to tell her that her appetite had nothing to do with her mental health.

Lying on her side with her back to the door of the room she was lucky enough not to have to share—hers was the only miscarriage that day and they *never* put new mothers in with almosts—Maggie counted the number of cars that turned into the hospital from the busy road that fronted it. There were very few at this time of night, visitors not being welcome unless they were family and the patient was critical.

She was alone for the duration.

Her nose twitched, followed by a distinct rumble from her stomach as the heady aroma defined itself as greasy hamburgers. One of the nurses must have brought in a snack, she decided, and seriously considered calling out for pizza.

If the delivery boy told them he was family, he just might get through.

She lay very still, pursuing multiple angles of the subject of food and access thereto with a fervor that reflected an inner desperation to think of something . . . *anything* . . . that didn't remind her of why she was lying in a hospital bed in the first place.

She steadfastly avoided adding to her journal. Outside of the technicality that the leather-bound book was at home and she wasn't, she couldn't bring herself to put down in black and white emotions that were too raw for comfort.

She didn't know if she ever could.

Food was merely the latest of a long line of busywork for her brain. In the last couple of hours, she'd mentally reorganized her kitchen and landscaped the grass and oleander bushes in her backyard into something that resembled an English walking garden. In a separate compartment of her mind she updated her résumé and composed a letter of resignation to her boss.

It was time for a change.

She'd even given serious thought to moving to Washington State, calculating how much she'd get for her house in Vacaville and how far that would take her in the booming real-estate market up north. It was a proposition worth considering, although she wasn't sure she was prepared to exchange California's almost irritatingly perfect weather for the beautiful but enduringly soggy climate of the Evergreen State.

Her stomach rumbled again. "Damn!" she muttered, wishing whoever it was with the food would hurry up and eat it before she did something totally foolish like offer a bribe for a small bite.

"I thought you were asleep."

She turned her head and saw him in the shadows

next to the open door. He was leaning against the wall, arms folded across his chest. Will. She should have known he would come.

But she hadn't. She hadn't dared to hope.

Now she had to do her best to make him stay. For what it was worth, she decided it would be nice if she didn't burst into tears. If Will was like most men, he'd panic and maybe even leave.

She couldn't bear that. Not yet.

"I brought you something," he said, not moving.

A paper bag with grease marks streaking the side dangled from his fingers. A clue.

"So you're the one who's been torturing me," she said, rolling carefully onto her back. She grimaced a little as she scooted up on the bed. "I'll have you know I've been fantasizing about what's in that sack. I bet I caught my first whiff of it the second you got off the elevator."

He pushed away from the wall and eased his way across the room, his unhurried movements comforting her nerves in a way she couldn't explain. He drew up the adjustable table from the foot of the bed, squaring it over her lap. She watched as he opened the bag and sorted out the contents. Hamburgers, fries, apple pies. Four of everything.

What was he going to eat?

"I'd turn on a light, but then they'd catch me and I'd have to leave," he said, his deep voice a soothing balm in the darkness.

"You snuck in?"

"Hmm."

"What if they smell the food?"

"I trust it won't be around long enough to give us away." He folded back the paper wrapper from a burger and pushed it toward her.

She stared at the sandwich, grateful for the darkness. Her complexion was testimony to every single tear she'd cried that day and if he said anything about it, she'd probably start crying all over again.

She tilted her head to look at him, but she saw only

shadows because his back was to the light. What was he thinking? she asked herself. Why had he come? Was it pity? Guilt?

She didn't want his guilt. "I wouldn't have told you—"

His fingers were suddenly on her lips, silencing her. "Not now, Maggie," he murmured. "Later. I need some time to slow down first."

"Slow down?" she said, her mouth brushing his fingers. She missed their warmth when they dropped away.

He nodded, the movement barely perceptible in the dim room. "It's been just over three hours since you called. I've covered a lot of territory since then—physically *and* emotionally." He paused. "I need to catch my breath."

Maggie could relate to that. She picked up the hamburger and took a bite. Oh my, but that tasted good! She chewed quickly and ate some more.

"You must be starving," he said. "Hospital food can't possibly be enough for a woman with your appetite."

"The pudding was good," she allowed, watching as he unwrapped another hamburger and bit into it. "But I hate stuffed peppers."

She thought she saw a faint smile cross his lips. "I'll bet that didn't stop you from eating them."

She almost smiled back. With a sigh that was only a little ragged, she relaxed what was left of her guard and concentrated on the feast he'd brought her.

After two hamburgers, a few dozen fries and one apple pie, Maggie thought she might survive until morning. Will was clearly incredulous when she declined her second apple pie. She watched as he pushed the meager leftovers into the bag and trashed it.

It was time.

"I didn't expect you to come," she said when he'd moved the table aside and resumed his place, his thigh nudging hers.

"I know."

"I'm glad," she said softly, fiddling with the edge of

her blanket as she tried to marshal her thoughts. "I wasn't having much luck being brave."

"Me neither."

She looked at him, surprised. In the wash of light from the street lamp beneath her window, she stared as a single tear tracked down his cheek. It was followed by another . . . and another. With a muffled cry, she buried her face in his shoulder, giving in to the tears she'd foolishly thought she could control.

Will folded his arms around Maggie and held her close to his heart. He rocked her and stroked her hair as she wept, whispering comforting noises that he knew she couldn't possibly understand. He told her that he loved her and then told her to blow into the tissue he held to her nose when she seemed to be having trouble breathing.

She sobbed against his shirt and he tightened his hold, trying so very hard to be strong for her. After a long time, her cries subsided. He still held her, gently rearranging their positions until he rested against the raised head of the bed and she lay in his arms. She calmed and, finally, she slept. He didn't let her go.

Staring blindly into the night, he kept the woman he loved safely in his arms. For the first time, he felt the wet tracks of tears on his own cheeks . . . and wondered when that had happened.

It was past midnight when the nurse counted two noses instead of one in Room 212.

Will waited in silence as the middle-aged woman stood at the door and glared at him. He'd figured someone would discover him sooner or later.

He just couldn't seem to give in gracefully, though. They were going to have to throw him out, he decided, and it was going to take more than one nurse to do it.

Stubbornly, he glared back at her.

She let out a soft, resigned sigh and crossed the room, silent on rubber soles.

He couldn't figure out how she planned to do it.

Besides outweighing the woman by a hundred pounds, give or take, he was solidly attached to Maggie, yet another hundred pounds of dead weight.

She walked around to the other side of the bed and took Maggie's wrist.

He tightened his hold on Maggie.

Laura Johnson was what was on her name tag. RN. He had to give her credit for clear thinking. She was going to wake Maggie and let her kick Will out.

But Maggie needed to rest. He had just decided to leave quietly when he realized Nurse Johnson was looking at her watch. She was taking Maggie's pulse.

He decided to wait and see. Not moving a muscle, he watched as the nurse gently slipped a blood-pressure sleeve onto Maggie's arm, taking care not to awaken her.

He'd just about relaxed when Nurse Laura Johnson lifted the thin blanket that covered Maggie and told him softly but firmly to hold it up. He did as he was told, and the blanket effectively shielded from his gaze whatever the nurse was doing to Maggie.

A few moments later the nurse snatched back the blanket, tucked it in, and said in a low voice. "I'll expect you to be gone before five. Doctors' rounds are at quarter to six."

"ᴀᴍ?" Somehow, it didn't seem fair.

Laura Johnson grinned. "I'll wake you."

"Come back to Tahoe with me." A loud clanging sounded out in the hall as Will spoke, lunch being served or whatever, and he had to say it again. "Come back to Tahoe with me, Maggie."

"Don't be silly." Maggie pulled on a pale-yellow cardigan over a silk shell and stuck her hands in the pockets of the matching light wool trousers. Will had done a remarkable job of bringing things from her closet that actually went together. "I've already made plans to go to the beach."

"You can't go all the way there alone. You're not fit to drive yet."

She smiled gently. "Matt will join me when he can."

"You forget that I was here when you talked to base ops on the phone. They don't know when your brother is due in."

"That's just because his plane is broken down somewhere out in the system. No one seems to know whether Matt left the crew with the plane and hitched a ride on another aircraft or what." A resigned sigh parted her lips.

"You told his squadron commander there was no hurry."

She nodded, ducking her head to avoid his accusing stare. She'd tried to downplay her predicament when she'd talked with Matt's squadron commander because, at the last moment, she'd realized she needed to be alone. Having a solicitous sibling around didn't match up with her recovery plans.

Will ground his teeth and tried reasoning with her. "The doctor says he'll only release you if there's someone to take care of you. Unless you go with me, you don't have anyone!"

"Shush!" Maggie snuck a peek out the door to make sure none of the doctor's spies had overheard. No one was lurking in the corridor. With an exaggerated sigh of relief, she turned back to Will, hands on her hips and ready to do battle. "If I have to stay here another minute, I'll starve to death and it'll all be *your* fault."

"You could still grab a lunch tray."

"I want *real* food." She patted her grumbling stomach. "The stuff they served for breakfast looked too pathetic to eat."

"That didn't stop you."

She grimaced. "You can at least give me credit for hesitating."

"You won't starve if you let me take care of you."

"I don't *want* to be taken care of," she said, easing the door halfway shut before turning back to glare at him. Her expression softened as she added, "Don't think I don't appreciate your coming last night, but I've got a handle on things now and I don't need a baby-sitter."

"The doctor says you do."

"He says I need rest."

"You can rest in Tahoe." Will was mildly surprised that he was using logic with Maggie "But then, he'd been surprised by a lot of things over the past few hours.

First there was her home. He'd only seen the outside before, but that morning, when he'd driven over to pick up some clothes and whatnot, he'd gone inside and really seen how she lived.

She lived very well. Maggie's home was spacious and comfortable and immaculate. He wondered how she could afford it on a receptionist's salary.

He had taken a few minutes to prowl through the rooms, an activity that raised more questions. He'd found a computer, a fancy one accompanied by a shelfful of books on various programming languages and tasks.

The Maggie he knew wouldn't know how to plug the electronic gadget into the wall, much less turn it on.

He'd found a library of sorts, really a sitting room filled with books. Lots of them. Books on geography and the origins of humanity. Books on wines and on furniture making in the nineteenth century. Books on stars and planets and moons that had nothing to do with astrology. Best-selling novels and award-winning mysteries.

The Maggie he knew had trouble reading a menu. In English.

A stereo headset was clipped over the arm of the most comfortable-looking chair in the room. He traced the cord backward and discovered a state-of-the-art stereo component system set inside a cabinet. Her collection of compact discs was impressive, her taste varying from Mariah Carey to Cole Porter to Andrew Lloyd Webber.

The Maggie he knew had once admitted to only liking music she could dance to.

Will found her bedroom and ceased prying, picking

up the few things she'd asked for and leaving without invading her privacy any further. Locking the front door as he left, he tried to feel guilty about snooping through her house, but dismissed the activity as natural curiosity.

Any man would be curious if the woman he loved was such an incredible contradiction. Fascinating, she was.

It had been puzzling him since breakfast, the way she was now as opposed to how she'd acted in Tahoe. She'd been calm and reasonably patient throughout the process of dealing with the hospital bureaucracy. She'd filled out forms, answered questions, and submitted to a final examination—all without expressing any of the ditzier sides of her personality.

Hovering in the hallway, Will hadn't heard her voice a single remark that could have been regarded as even slightly airheaded. It occurred to him that perhaps she hadn't changed at all. He was just getting used to it.

He was worried that he wasn't worried.

"I don't want to go to Tahoe," Maggie said, breaking into his thoughts as she gathered her things from around the room and stuffed them into the nylon bag he'd brought. "Besides the fact it's a long drive—"

"We'll fly," he cut in. "I've got the plane waiting for us now. We can be there in time for a late lunch."

"You flew down last night?"

He nodded. "I was in a hurry. As it was, most of the time was spent hunting up a pilot and then finding out which hospital you were in—not to mention the detour for food." He nearly hadn't made it that quickly. His pilot had gone missing—probably hiking or camping or whatever he usually did on vacation time—and Will had just decided to fly the plane himself when Biff somehow caught wind of his plans.

Biff, it seemed, was a pilot too—something else Will hadn't known about him. On the short flight to Vacaville, Will had found himself telling the younger man the reason for the trip.

He hadn't been surprised that Biff remembered Maggie. Everyone remembered Maggie. He'd been astonished, though, when Biff admonished him for not going to her sooner.

It was like fishing, Biff explained. A good fisherman knows which ones to keep and which ones to return to the water. Maggie was definitely a keeper. Even Biff knew that, and he'd only talked with her a couple of times.

Obviously, Will wasn't much of a fisherman.

He was beginning to agree.

The computer. Her books. The music. Long periods of apparent rationality. The incongruities were free associating at such a frantic pace, he decided his mind was playing tricks on him.

"You might not have noticed," he told her, "but I was here just three hours after you called. It takes at least four to get to Tahoe by road."

"And here I thought you were merely living up to your reputation," she said sweetly.

"Reputation?"

She grinned. "Don't you know that truck drivers are known to really boogie?"

"Boogie?"

"Speed. Drive fast." Maggie laughed at the helpless expression on his face and was proud of herself for incurring its return. She'd been too long out of character, too close to exposing the real Maggie.

That would never do.

The computer. Her books. The music. Wasn't it just a tad condescending to think Maggie wouldn't know how to boot up a computer?

"I'm not a truck driver. Understand?" He put his hands on her shoulders and squeezed as though he could transmit the information that way.

She smiled.

Somehow, he didn't feel relieved. "What about it, Maggie? Will you come to Tahoe with me?"

Maggie hesitated. His hands were so warm on her shoulders, his strength tempered by a gentleness she as fast becoming addicted to. Last night she'd needed is strength, his gentleness, his words of comfort and ve.

It hadn't computed when he said he loved her, not 1en. But this morning, when she awakened to find erself alone, it had been the first thing she'd remem- ered of the night before.

He'd said *I love you, Maggie.* Right after that, she emembered blowing her nose into the tissue he held.

Such a romantic response.

It made remembering easier, though, because if she'd esponded with her own words of love this morning vould be fraught with tension instead of the easy ompanionship they'd shared the last few hours. She vas very much afraid that he'd only said what he did ut of comfort.

Blowing her nose had saved her pride.

Going to Tahoe was entirely too dangerous to con- emplate. Despite her initial good spirits that morning, he hospital psychiatrist had warned her to beware of almost guaranteed setbacks. It followed that being anywhere near Will was not a good idea. With him around, she knew she'd rely less on her own powers of ecovery and more on him.

She couldn't afford to let it become a habit. Will was 1ot a permanent part of her life—just someone who was bassing through. She didn't want to lean on someone who wouldn't be there two days or even two months rom now.

She didn't want to lean on anyone at all.

Besides, he'd already done so much for her. Because of Will she finally had confidence in the sensual side of her nature. But that accomplishment was only part one of the two-part renovation she'd planned.

Between doctors' visits, filling out forms, and prepar- ing her aching body to leave the hospital, Maggie had decided not to tell him about part two. It was out of character to have a driving need to do something fulfilling with her life. Mixed-up Maggie or Bambi Bub-

blehead would equate a career with keeping a job long
enough to earn vacation time. It wouldn't occur to her
to question how gratifying it was as long as it wasn't too
strenuous and didn't require overtime.

At the moment, she wished to hell she'd never created
the airhead alter ego.

She felt his hands tighten gently on her shoulders
and knew she'd been spaced-out for more than a short
while. No matter, she thought. Will was used to her
eccentricities by now.

"I can't go to Tahoe with you, Will," she said gently. "I
need some time to put my life back together and
returning to the scene of the crime, so to speak, isn't
exactly what I think I should do."

"I want to take care of you," he insisted, unconcerned
that he was repeating himself.

Tears formed in her eyes and she had to swallow
before speaking. "I loved my baby," she said quietly. "I
need to come to grips with what happened."

"It happened to me too," he said just as softly. "Please
come."

"Can't." She sniffled and shook her head, then said
the first thing that came into her head. "I, um . . . I
promised my brother I'd show him how to program the
computer to keep track of his squadron's training
schedules. Seems they're stuck with a program designed by some guy at another base and it doesn't work
at all."

What the hell did Maggie know about programming? Will asked himself. *Computer. Books. Music.* He
pushed the swirling paradox aside because she was
slipping away from him and he had to work fast to stop
her.

"Maggie?"

"Yes?"

"What if I said I was in love with you? Would you
come with me then?"

Her breath caught in her throat. She'd thought he'd
said that only to comfort. Obviously, it was more

serious than that. Will Jackson wasn't a man to say anything he absolutely did not mean.

Her stomach clenched with the disquieting discovery that something wholly unforeseen had happened.

"Are you sure?" she asked.

He nodded.

Nine

"You fell in love with that twit?"

"What twit?" Will wondered if this was another truck driver maze.

"Bambi Bubblehead, of course!" she sputtered, easing off the bed before he could reach out to help her. Taking careful steps, she began pacing in the confined space. "I can't believe this!"

He blocked her stride and grabbed her by the arms. "Who the hell is Bambi Bubblehead?"

"The woman you're in love with." Shrugging off his hands, she backed up against the wall. "And here I thought you were a reasonably intelligent man!"

"That's certainly not an assumption anyone could make about you!" His hands fisted at his sides in total and absolute frustration. *Who the hell was Bambi Bubblehead?*

Maggie gritted her teeth and refused to rise to that last crack. He was ninety-nine percent right—from his point of view, of course. Of all the complications she'd anticipated when she planned this undertaking, *this* was not one of them.

The computer, her books, the music . . . Bambi Bub-

blehead. The inconsistencies fell into place with a logic that was almost brazen, once Will had all the pieces. Maggie was no more a ditzy blonde than he was.

He tracked her retreat. When it looked as though she might duck outside, he barred her way by flattening his hands on the wall on either side of her head. "We can do this standing or sitting," he said, "but either way, you're going to come clean, Maggie love."

"Come clean?" she squeaked, suddenly realizing that her indignant outburst had raised certain questions of duplicity. She made a stab at retrenching. "But you know I just took a shower!"

His gaze narrowed in warning. "No more games, Maggie."

She sighed. "No games," she agreed, giving up the pretense with a reluctant concession to survival. "It was never a game."

"Then why the act?" he asked, his voice knife smooth and so low she had to strain to hear. "Or is there a particular reason you thought I'd prefer a dumb blonde to—" Will shrugged, totally incapable of filling in the blank.

"I prefer the term bubblehead," she said.

"There's a difference?"

She had the audacity to look affronted. "I was *never* a dumb blonde. A little scatterbrained, perhaps, but never dumb. Strictly speaking, dumb is defined as incapable of speech."

He almost laughed, but he refrained. He wasn't going to let her off the hook that easily. Thanks to many years' experience in hiding his emotions during business negotiations, he was now able to keep from showing Maggie how close he was to laughter.

Maggie felt his hands move onto her shoulders and slide toward her neck—a better position from which to strangle her, she imagined. Long fingers worked their way around her throat, settling there with only the slightest pressure. She wasn't worried. Will wouldn't hurt her, not with his hands.

It was the intensely threatening look in his eyes that

was going to do the damage. It surprised her that she couldn't actually feel the bite of steel she saw in his gaze. She almost wilted under his unwavering stare, but she was made of sterner stuff. She hoped.

"Why the act?" he asked again. "Are you so smart that you frighten men off?"

She blinked, and barely kept herself from smiling at his curious leap in logic. Talk about extremes! "It wasn't that," she said evenly. "In the normal course of a day, I manage to communicate with most men without threatening their egos."

Will could see the smile in her eyes, the confidence that she wasn't the least bit intimidated by him. He was inordinately pleased by that. She wasn't afraid. She trusted him.

He wasn't ready to be teased and cajoled yet, though. With precise movements, he removed his hands from her throat. He led her back to the bed and gently lifted her to sit on it.

He left her there, moving away to look out the window. "Tell me, Maggie. Tell me all of it. Why the dumb blonde routine?"

"Bubblehead."

"Whatever." His voice sharpened with impatience.

"The idea of seducing a man was pretty scary, given my background," she said. "I was worried that I'd laugh at the wrong time or say something that would show that I really didn't know what I was doing. I figured I'd be able to cover up a lot if I played it a little loony."

A *little* loony, he repeated silently, but let that one go. He knew he could tease her about it anytime. "All this because your husband left you with a few hang-ups."

She nodded. "Charles told me that I was sexless and inhibited and cold—"

"He what?" Will spun to face her.

Maggie grimaced and blushed to the roots of her hair. "I am *not* going to repeat that," she said firmly, glancing up to see the disbelief in his eyes. She was reassured enough to give him a tiny smile. "It's embarrassing enough to admit that I believed him."

"Those were his exact words?"

"Among others. Those are just the ones I remember best."

"He was a fool," Will said succinctly.

"That thought has occurred to me since we, er, since we—"

"Since we made love and you discovered what an incredibly sensual woman you really are," he finished for her, and delighted in her deepening color.

A tiny moan of remembered passion left her lips. "Something like that."

"I should be absolutely furious with you, you know," he said, admiring the way she sat there without a hint of chagrin at getting caught.

"Because I'm not a dumb blonde?"

He shook his head slowly, finally letting a smile touch his lips. "Because you didn't tell me sooner. I should have thought that once you were over that first hurdle—the first time we made love—that you might have realized you didn't need to pretend anything."

"In case you didn't notice," she said, then stopped to clear the huskiness from her voice, "Bambi Bubblehead didn't surface again until the next afternoon."

"If my memory serves me correctly, I think we were both too distracted that night to notice much of anything."

She blushed again, and wondered if she'd ever get over her schoolgirl reactions when she thought of those nights in Will's arms. Perhaps with a bit of repetition . . . She shook her head briskly, telling herself not to hope for the impossible.

She couldn't accept his invitation to Tahoe. It was too dangerous, too foolhardy even to contemplate.

He'd said he loved her . . . but how could he when he didn't know her? Would he even like the woman she really was?

Her newfound confidence didn't extend that far.

She took a deep breath and said, "I suppose I should be offended you didn't guess."

"That you were a fraud?" He shook his head. "Sorry,

Maggie. I was too busy enjoying you to dissect the discrepancies."

"Maybe that's why I didn't say anything," she said softly. "I didn't want it to end."

Those were the words he'd been waiting for. "I've never been in love before," he said. "I'm not sure I like being told I've fallen for a twit."

"I can appreciate that," she joked, uneasy with his earnest countenance. "Your ego would be suspect if you weren't a little miffed."

"And you think that now that I know, I'll just give up?"

She nodded, a little sadly. "I'm not a twit and I'm not a beautiful seductress. I'm just plain Maggie Cooper who lives in Vacaville and can't ski worth a damn."

She couldn't bear to look at him and see the confirmation in his eyes. She stared at her hands instead, and wished the doctor would hurry up and dismiss her before she made a fool out of herself and told Will that just plain Maggie Cooper loved him very much.

Or thought she did. To tell the truth, Maggie wasn't certain of anything right now. She'd thought of little else but Will since leaving Tahoe, more so when she'd realized she was pregnant. The fact that those tender feelings were magnified the moment she knew she was carrying his baby had made her suspicious of them.

Did she love Will, or did she merely want to love the father of her child? She had asked herself the question so much over the course of her pregnancy, she'd nearly gone mad with not knowing.

She still didn't know.

"Do you think plain Maggie Cooper would like to come with me to Tahoe anyway?" Will asked softly.

Her head jerked up and she found her gaze caught by his. "Why?"

"Because I love her, and I want the chance to prove it to her."

Her heart stopped beating for as long as it took for her to realize he was serious. When it started again, its staccato rhythm betrayed her excitement . . . her anticipation that there were happy endings after all.

"What happens if she believes you?" she whispered.

Will left the window and came to her. Taking her trembling hands in his, he sat beside her on the bed. "Then, Maggie, I don't see any reason we shouldn't be together. Like we're supposed to be." A huge sigh gusted out as the tension of the last few minutes left his body. "It's what I want more than anything in the world."

"You're saying you want more than a fling?"

He nodded. "I want to be with you and share your days and nights. I want to learn everything there is to know about you. I want the chance to love you." He squeezed her hands and offered her the only thing he knew how to give. "A relationship, Maggie. Please don't say no without thinking about it. I know we'll be good together."

A relationship. She swallowed her disappointment, mentally kicking herself for allowing herself to wish for more than he had to offer.

"This is quite a switch," she said lightly. "You didn't want anything to do with a relationship when we first met."

"Neither did you," he pointed out. "I was merely being practical because you live in Vacaville. It didn't make sense. If you come to Tahoe, it will be the only thing that *does* make sense."

His argument was logical if a bit arrogant. Maggie didn't mind. She could be arrogant too, given the chance.

"What's your excuse for saying you didn't want one?" he asked, hugging her closer to his side.

It's what you wanted to hear, she almost said. Instead she mumbled, "Pretty much the same."

She was going to agree, Will thought. He could feel her resistance ebbing, knew that the most important thing he'd ever wanted in his life was within his grasp.

Yet he knew he had to say the words that might make her decide against it. Raising her chin with the knuckles of one hand, he said softly, "I don't believe in marriage, Maggie."

She nodded. "I know that." And just because she didn't agree didn't mean she had to tell him about it.

His gaze held hers for a long moment until he was apparently satisfied. "As long as you understand."

She let him believe whatever he wanted.

"So you'll come with me?" he asked yet again. He knew he'd keep asking until she said yes.

"What about Bambi?" she asked.

"She can come too," he said, grinning at her exasperation. "I kind of miss her." He lifted her hands to kiss her fingers, one by one. Slipping an arm around her shoulders, he pulled her against him, needing the warmth of her body as a physical reassurance that she was there and not a dream.

Maggie's mind raced over the ramifications of what he'd just offered her. A relationship. A thing of terminal dimensions. A relationship because Will didn't believe in marriage.

I'll never marry. Not ever.

She had no reason to doubt him. But just as she didn't know why she loved Will, she couldn't quite believe he intended to go through his life alone and unattached. The notion reeked of a loneliness that was all too close to home.

She cared for him too much to want him to be lonely.

I'll never marry. Not ever.

As a wise man once told her, never say never. She almost laughed aloud, remembering the skiing disaster and Will's determination that she not give up. The next image was of the two of them, laughing again as they had the last winter. Loving.

But if she really did fall in love—for all the right reasons—would a relationship be enough for her? Maggie felt the warmth of his body next to hers, and knew that it might have to be.

Might.

"Will?"

"Yes?" he said, brushing a wisp of hair from her forehead before planting a kiss in its place.

"Keeping in mind that I haven't agreed to anything yet, what happens to this relationship if I don't fall in love with you?" She remembered clearly that she'd not said a word aloud about her own feelings.

He took her chin in his fingers, holding her captive for his study. After a long moment, he leaned forward and kissed her lips. She waited, her gaze arrested by his, her heart thumping loudly in her chest.

"Maggie love, I can see it in your eyes. You already have."

Maggie's next trip to Tahoe took considerably more planning than the first. She had to quit her job, find a realtor to rent out her house, and tidy up all the details involved in leaving a place for a substantial period of time.

She had to pack away the baby books too, the ones she'd bought with such bright hopes just weeks before. That hadn't occurred to her before, not until she stumbled across the first one.

She was alone when she found it. Will had gone out "foraging for dinner," or to the grocery store if all else failed. And just the day before, Matt had flown off into the wild blue yonder—Alaska and points west, to be precise.

She hadn't been looking, but there it was all the same, tucked in her bedside drawer beneath the telephone book. On the cover was a delicate portrait of cherubs sitting on pastel clouds. Inside were hundreds of suggestions for names, boys' and girls'.

Clutching the book in both hands, she sank down onto the bed and wept.

It was a first for Maggie. In the days since she'd left the hospital, she'd made a point of saving her tears for the night. During the day she tried to be brave, to think of anything else so that she could go on with a normal life and not have to stop and wait for her eyes to clear so she could see again. She'd convinced herself that if she could make it through the day without crying, it was surely a sign that she was getting over it.

Since Will was sleeping in the guest room, she kept her tears to herself. She hadn't wanted to sleep apart, but he'd been insistent. Her double bed was too small for the two of them, he said. He might roll over and hurt her.

"Too late," she'd quipped sharply, hurt by the distance he was putting between them. "The damage is already done."

He'd pulled her into his arms and stroked her hair, telling her everything would be all right. Soon they'd be sleeping together again, as it should be.

And she'd get over it. Perhaps not right away, but someday.

She'd believed him, just as she'd realized she had to rely on herself to get through this. Not because Will wasn't there for her now, but because he might not be at some point down the line. What use was it to depend on someone who might disappear any day?

It made sense, yet it filled her with an uncomfortable sense of dread. Life without Will wasn't something she wanted to contemplate.

Maggie stared through tear-filled eyes at the volume of children's names in her hands and knew suddenly that she'd never get over it. It was inconceivable to believe her heart would heal, that she'd ever be able to think of the child she'd *never even held* and not cry. Will's child, the baby they'd made together.

Will's child, the baby she'd wanted more than anything on earth.

The tears were still falling when she felt his arms enfold her. She resisted, sniffling back the tears, blasting her senses for not being aware that he'd returned.

Time to be brave. "Sorry about that," she said, wiping her cheeks with the back of her hand. "Guess I miss Matt more than I thought." Edging away, she tucked the book under her thigh and prayed he hadn't seen it. "Matt likes you, you know."

"I like Matt too," Will said, his gaze gentle on her tear-stained face. "I just wish he hadn't had to punch me before figuring that out."

Maggie relaxed a little, realizing her tactic had worked. "Big brother protecting little sister. It would have helped if I'd told him I was pregnant and how before everything fell apart."

"The 'how' isn't any of his business," Will said, then his voice dropped to a husky murmur. "I remember exactly how it happened. It was the first night we were together. I rolled over, pulled you into my arms, and took you without hardly any warning at all. The last thing on my mind was taking precautions."

"That's not the 'how' I was referring to," she said, blushing furiously. He talked so easily about making love . . . as easily as most people discussed the weather! "I meant the part about me seducing you. As it was, he kind of put the blame on you."

Will shook his head and shifted until he could actually hold her. This time, she let him. He pulled her into the circle of his arms, gently pushed her face against his chest so that she could hear the steady beat of his heart . . . and tugged the book out from under her thigh. He looked at it briefly, then tossed it onto the bed.

She felt herself go limp when he didn't mention it.

She finally relaxed against him, her own arms snaking around his waist as he stroked her hair. "There's no one to *blame* for anything. We made love. We made a baby. We lost it. No one did anything wrong, Maggie. You have to quit beating yourself up for something you didn't do."

So much for thinking he wasn't going to talk about it.

"I could have been more careful," she said, the tears she'd so recently stopped now wetting his shirt. "If I hadn't fallen—"

"You could have stayed in bed for nine months and still lost it." Cupping her chin so that she would meet his gaze, he said, "You didn't do anything wrong, Maggie."

"Then why can't I stop crying?"

"Maybe you just need to share your tears," he murmured, his lips moving across the wetness that blanketed her cheeks.

"But you won't sleep with me—"

He hushed her with his lips. "And who says you have to save your tears for the nights? Cry with me, love. Let the grief go before it becomes too much to handle. Cry with me and let it go."

Cry with me and let it go.

Share, he'd said. Not lean on, not depend, just share. Love. Was that why it was so easy to do as he asked?

Somehow, everything was easier after that afternoon. Maggie still cried at the drop of a hat, but after a few weeks, the hat seemed to drop less often.

She concentrated on her impending move and all that went with it. It took a mere six weeks to get all her ducks into line. She was pleased everything fell into place so easily.

Will was ready to shoot those ducks and any other excuse by the end of those six weeks. He returned to Tahoe after the first week and called every night, visited most weekends, and generally made a nuisance of himself until Maggie told him—point blank—that if he didn't stop pushing, she'd possibly have to rethink the whole adventure. After all, it was her life that was being disrupted, not his.

He backed off, wondering how she could possibly imagine that his life wasn't in total chaos. Without Maggie at his side, everyone suffered. His moods swung from the exhilaration of knowing she was coming to despair that she was taking her damn time about it!

Their weekends were spent talking, organizing, and packing. He asked what kind of job she intended to find once she *finally* got to the mountains, and she told him that anything would do as long as she'd never done it before. He was surprised, because from what he'd heard about the job she'd just quit, she took pride in her work.

She shrugged it off and said she'd been a terrific waitress at one point in her life, but that didn't mean she wanted to do it forever. When he asked what other jobs she'd held, she told him she'd been an executive secretary in an insurance brokerage during the two years she attended night school. After that, she'd landed a job as a cost estimator for a firm that made small parts for a couple of airplane manufacturers. No experience required, they'd said, and while it was challenging work, it just wasn't for her.

Then there was the six months she'd spent selling condominiums. That hadn't worked out at all because Maggie could no more sell anything than she could ski The Face at Heavenly. She'd been office manager at the accounting firm for over a year, but was more than ready to move on.

She kept her tone nonchalant and easy, determined not to reveal her vulnerability on this subject. She knew how persistent Will could be when he sensed that she wasn't sharing everything. How could she tell him that yes, she wanted to be a writer, but *let's get real here*?

She didn't trust him enough to share the fantasy. Or, perhaps, she was saving that piece of herself against the day when she might have to salvage something important that she hadn't given away.

It had happened before. She tried not to worry about it.

Will admired the fact that Maggie was willing to try her hand at just about anything. After discussing the matter with Casey, he arrived the following weekend with a list of positions currently vacant within the hotel. Maggie asked if it would be all right if she tried the one that was available in the catering department—provided, of course, that the catering manager, Angelo DiPietro, was willing.

Will had to physically sit on his hands to keep from interfering. After a telephone interview, Maggie was offered the job as assistant to the catering manager and DiPietro sounded pleased about it. Maggie could only hope that this was what she was looking for.

Their discussions about where she would live were lively. He wanted her in his home, which was just a few miles east of town on the Nevada side of the lake. She was equally as adamant about finding an apartment—a small one, because she'd decided to rent her house furnished. Thanks to the nearby military base, there were always people who needed a place for just a few months and who didn't want to bother moving in their own things.

Will had never asked a woman to live with him. He wanted her to know this wasn't something he did on a whim.

Maggie couldn't imagine living with a man to whom she wasn't married. She told him so and he stopped insisting.

He didn't want her to be isolated in an apartment with no one aware of her comings and goings. The weather was too severe in Tahoe. He'd drive her nuts with worrying about her.

She wasn't crazy about that either—the apartment or his worrying—but she didn't see any other solution.

He did. There was an apartment attached to the hotel, which had been designed for a live-in manager. It was vacant at present, since Casey was the manager and he and Harriet preferred to live in a home they'd purchased nearby.

Maggie agreed.

They argued about the rent until Will put down his foot and said he couldn't accept payment for something that wasn't bringing in any revenue anyway. She agreed again, knowing it was a temporary solution at best.

Then there was the night her tongue ran away from her and she said the one thing she'd sworn she wouldn't ever say.

"I never asked you if you wanted to have children."

A bolt of shock flashed through Will as she voiced the quandary he'd dodged for the past month. Shifting her in his arms, he stroked her hair and hoped she wouldn't pursue it. He didn't have a clue how to answer her.

He liked children, but had never allowed himself to imagine having any of his own. After all, his antimarriage stance naturally precluded the family image and all that went along with it. But when she'd miscarried the child they'd made together, it had exposed a longing that was as unfamiliar as it was intense.

He wanted a child.

He wanted to nurture and teach and protect a human being that he'd had a part in creating.

He could just imagine asking Maggie if she would like to have a child with him—keeping in mind, of course, that marriage was out of the question. Utter nonsense.

"Will?" Maggie elbowed her way out of his arms until they were wrapped loosely around her waist and she could see his somber expression. "Did you hear me?"

He swallowed and looked over her shoulder. He didn't want to see her face because he didn't want to know if she liked his response or not. "I heard you, Maggie. I'm afraid I just don't have a good answer for you right now."

"Why's that?"

"Because as much as I regret that you lost the baby, I've always felt a child deserves both a mother and a father." And then, because he didn't want her to have any false illusions, he looked at her and said, "A married mother and father. And I've told you how I feel about marriage."

Maggie nodded and filed that away.

One step at a time.

Six weeks, ducks in a line, and Will was gunning for them. She smiled at his impatience because it made the trip to Lake Tahoe all the more exciting.

It was a changed Maggie who steered the little orange

car through the hairpins and other vicious curves. They were a challenge even though the mid-September weather was mild and dry. The grief that had almost overwhelmed her during the days and weeks following her miscarriage still tugged at her emotions, bringing tears at odd moments when she remembered what might have been. Still, she was okay now, and she knew it.

Will knew it too. Every night when they talked on the phone, he verbally poked and prodded until he was convinced she wasn't holding back on him.

Life went on, and she was ready to get on with it. Ready and willing—because she had a secret Will hadn't tumbled to yet.

Maggie grinned as she reached a passing lane, pulling to the right so the dozen or so supercharged automobiles behind her could skate by. Gearing down to compensate for the steeper grade, she wondered how long she'd have before Will found her out.

He already knew she was falling in love with him. He didn't know that she was quite done with the falling. She was totally, unequivocally, *happily* in love. There was no longer any confusion in her heart about how or why.

She loved Will for Will and that was that.

She hummed a tune under her breath and wondered how long it was going to take her to convince him that marriage was the only logical solution to the feelings between them. He'd resist her, she knew, and for that reason she didn't intend to bring it up at all.

She'd wait for him to figure it out all by himself.

Flinging the Volkswagen around a thirty-degree turn with only a slight screech of rubber against road, she laughed aloud and wondered if her patience quotient was up for what might be a very long wait.

Ten

The last time Maggie remembered being best buddies with a member of the opposite sex was back in junior high when Harry Franklin from next door conned her into sneaking out after midnight in order to obtain blackmail-quality photos of his sister, who was dating a particularly scuzzy halfback from a rival high school's football team.

From the moment she arrived in Tahoe, Maggie felt like she'd been a whole lot closer to Harry than she was to Will.

Granted, it had been two weeks since she'd last seen him, and nearly six months since their first meeting. It made sense that he might be a little hesitant toward her.

The bear hug he gave her in the parking lot wasn't so much hesitant as it was, well, *friendly*.

A bear hug, and not a kiss.

She was confounded by his attitude, so much so that she merely stood by as he helped the bellman load the contents of her car onto a couple of rolling carts. He teased her about what she considered too fragile to have left for the movers to handle, and surprised her with an offer to help her unpack—after she rested, of course. It had been a long drive and he didn't want her to get overtired.

She wanted him to kiss her and all he wanted her to do was nap.

She was ready to scream.

Not that there was anything concrete she could complain about. Will was a model of solicitous amiability. He returned to her apartment after what he thought was an appropriate length of time for her nap to help her unpack. He hefted the suitcases and positioned them for easy unloading in between showing off the amenities of the one-bedroom apartment, which included new cabinets and desks to accommodate the electronic equipment she'd insisted on bringing.

Then he took her to dinner where he spent the bulk of the meal introducing her to or pointing out staff members, as well as giving her a detailed breakdown of the various departments and their responsibilities.

He was making her crazy.

She waited impatiently for him to look at her in the way he did when all he wanted was to make long, fiery love to her. He didn't, and she began to wonder if the six months apart had weakened the flame that had once burned between them.

Casey sat down with them for a time, and Maggie realized that while Will might "own the place," as he'd once described it, he was more than willing to let Casey manage as he saw fit. Will, it seemed, was already busy with the responsibilities of several other business ventures, real estate being just one of them. Maggie wanted to know it all, not so much the facts about him now as the story of how he got there. The subject fascinated her. When Will grew bored of answering her questions about himself, she had no hesitation in asking Casey. He was only too pleased to tell her every little thing she wanted to know.

Will put up with it to a point, but when Casey began a much embellished version of last spring's Old Gee-

zers' Slalom Race, he excused Casey from the table with
threats of revenge if he didn't take the hint.

Casey got up to leave, but only because he'd just been
summoned to the reception desk. He wasn't, he told
Maggie, intimidated by a man who needed two skis to
finish a race when Casey had beat him out of second
place with only one.

After Casey finally left, Will attempted to shift the
conversation from his business to items of local interest. Maggie countered with the news that the doctor
had given her a clean bill of health two days earlier, just
to see if she could shatter his increasingly unbearable
calm.

It didn't work.

"Is there anything you can't do?" he asked almost
indifferently, shuttering his eyes from her probing gaze.

She shook her head.

He nodded briskly and said he was relieved, of
course, happy to know she hadn't suffered any physical
setbacks. Then he went on with his discussion about
the differences between South Lake Tahoe, California,
and Stateline, Nevada—the two towns that were theo-
retically separate yet physically joined, casino gam-
bling on the Nevada side being the prime distinction.

It was as if she'd told him she'd had to cut her hair a
quarter inch, but felt better about it now.

She seethed at his indifference, and wondered why
the hell he'd wanted her to come to Tahoe in the first
place—unless it was out of some misplaced feeling of
guilt. She was about to confront him on it when he told
her that DiPietro was hoping she'd be able to report for
work the day after tomorrow.

"I'd rather get started right away," she said, pushing
vegetables around her plate with her fork. Might as
well, she thought. Nothing better to do. Had the time
apart made him realize that all the emotions surrounding
her miscarriage were merely that—emotions, not love?

Had he forgotten how hot the flames of desire had
once burned between them?

"No," he said firmly, and her hopeful gaze clashed

with his bland one. She realized with almost over-whelming disappointment that he was talking about her job. "You'll have enough to do with getting settled in. In the meantime, I'd appreciate it if you'd concentrate on finishing your dinner. There's something I need to do."

Suddenly, without warning, fire flared in his eyes—the kind of fire she'd been waiting for. The kind she remembered.

"What?" she asked, her voice a whisper that couldn't possibly be heard over her thudding heart.

He leaned across the table and murmured, "Something intimate."

She couldn't eat another bite. She'd lost her appetite the moment the fire had returned and was pretty sure that was a first for her—losing her appetite, that is. She swallowed hard over the kind of dry-mouth, thumping-heart excitement his gaze effected, lost herself in a feeling so incredibly sensual, she could only wonder that she'd ever doubted.

He wanted her. She gloried in his need, his passion. His gaze heated as her own excitement transmitted itself to him. He threw down his napkin before reaching out a hand that she could have sworn trembled as he helped her to stand.

Then he became so coolly distant that were it not for the fact he was gently urging her toward the exit, she could have sworn he'd almost forgotten her existence.

"Give Biff a call when your things arrive tomorrow," he said, nodding a greeting at a couple that exited the elevator. With a hand at the small of her back, he guided her inside and punched the button for the third floor. "He said he'd come by and give you a hand with the movers, just in case. Sorry I can't be there myself, but I have to fly over to Reno in the morning and I won't be back before dinner."

"Outside of dropping the stereo or computer equipment, I wouldn't think there's much chance of anything going wrong," she said, leaning into his hand because it seemed it was the only contact she was to be allowed.

She was wrong.

He touched her chin with his fingers, lifting her face to his. "Promise me you'll call him."

"Promise," she murmured, her gaze locked on the mouth that hovered just inches from hers.

The elevator doors opened, and he withdrew, guiding her again with the excruciatingly minimal touch of his hand. Down a long hallway, around one corner and another, until they were in the isolated vestibule that fronted her apartment. He stopped so abruptly that one moment she felt his hand at her back and the next, all she knew was the touch of silk skirt against her knees, the coolness of the camisole that rested lightly on her breasts.

She spun abruptly, spooked by the notion that she'd see only his back as he retreated down the hall. But he was still there, just inches away, his gaze fixed on her mouth and his hands closing in to rest on her hips. She breathed a sigh of relief, and knew that her breath touched his lips because his fingers tightened on her in instant reaction.

"Are you going to be like this all the time?" she asked softly.

"Like what?"

"Blowing hot and cold and lukewarm until I don't know what to expect from you next."

Desire stole nearly all the color from his eyes. She felt herself floating, then drowning in the pools of black as he dragged her forward until her belly cushioned his hard arousal.

"You shouldn't have told me like that, Maggie. Right in the middle of dinner, like it wasn't anything more important than a trip to the park." His voice was husky, accusing, and aroused.

"Told you what?" she asked. But she knew, had known then what it would do to him. That's why she'd done it, though with seemingly indifferent results.

But he wasn't indifferent, she rejoiced, her hands coming up to rest on his arms, her fingers digging into the muscle there.

"About the doctor," he said. "It was all I could do no to haul you out of your chair right then, take you to th nearest closet—" He bit off the words with a curse, the bowed his head to test the shell of her ear. There wa nothing teasing about the aggressive way his tongu delved inside, retreating only so that his teeth coul fasten onto the soft lobe.

The assault left her weak and gasping. As if h sensed she was ready to collapse, he wrapped an arn around her waist, backing her against the wall so tha he could lean into her. "If I'd known this afternoon, w wouldn't have made it to dinner. Why didn't you tell m over the phone two days ago when you found out?"

"It wasn't exactly something I could just blurt out, she said dryly.

"But you did it anyway. You waited for the mos unlikely moment—practically the only time all day w weren't completely alone." He muttered promises c retribution that were shockingly arousing, then tool her mouth in a kiss as wild as any she'd ever experi enced.

"I couldn't help it," she said, panting a little. "Yo were acting so weird—like I was your buddy, not you lover."

"I was concentrating on keeping my hands off you How was I to know you could safely make love?"

"It was a great act," she told him. "You certainly ha me believing it."

"Maggie, you've never stopped being my lover, he said softly, covering her face with kisses as his bod shifted restlessly against hers. "Every night for the las six months, you've been with me. Even though yo were miles away, you were beside me, making me swea and hurt until the only sleep I got was when I finall convinced myself that you're coming back."

She smiled and said, "I'm back."

"Come closer."

Those were the first words he'd spoken since they'

out her apartment door between them and the world. He'd been insistent that they move inside. He wanted more than a kiss in the dark hallway.

He wanted to make love to her.

He was standing in a pool of light beside the dresser. It was the only light in the room because he'd turned off all the others the minute they'd finally managed to unclench long enough to come inside.

It hadn't been easy. In his arms, with his mouth gently forcing total recall, his hands drawing from her moans that expressed all the passion she'd saved for him—she would have made love with him anywhere.

He'd insisted they try the bedroom first.

She could see herself in the mirror above the dresser, but only in an unfocused sort of way. The violet shades of her blouse and skirt were illusionist smudges on the periphery of her vision. Her gaze was settled on the man who waited for her there.

He was completely, gloriously nude.

She hesitated, swaying on her feet as her senses were bombarded by the strength of his arousal, the masculine scent of him—the undisguised look of desire in his eyes.

"Closer."

She took a deep, fortifying breath and moved to stand in front of him. Touching . . . kissing distance. She couldn't resist. Lifting her hands, she placed them on his chest.

His heart fluttered against her palms before settling down to a hard, steady rhythm. She smiled, tilting her head back so that he could see it.

He wasn't smiling. "More," he demanded. "I want your hands all over me."

She noticed at last that his own hands were fisted at his sides. "You're not going to touch me?"

He groaned and shook his head. "Not yet."

"Why?"

"Because I want you to know something."

"Know what?"

"That you arouse me." That wasn't right, so Will tried

again. "I need you to know that you give me mor
pleasure than I've ever known in my entire life." H
sucked in his breath as her hands began to wande
over his chest, fingertips homing in on his small nip
ples, toying with them as she feathered light kisses al
around.

"Why is that so important?" she asked softly, widen
ing her strokes to include his belly button, dragging he
fingers across the slight ridge of curling hair that sh
encountered a few inches lower.

He took several deep breaths, but it wasn't until sh
shifted her level of exploration momentarily upwar
that he could answer. "Because it's not something yo
knew before you left," he said harshly. "We shared ou
pleasure, but I never let you discover how deeply yo
affected me."

She was perplexed that he was so determined to b
serious about something that didn't seem all that eartl
shattering. She had known that she gave him pleasure
known and appreciated the significance. Without tha
knowledge, her own sensual discovery would have bee
an empty victory indeed.

"What makes you think I didn't know?"

"You wouldn't have left," he said simply. And then
taking her hand, he urged her to touch his throbbin,
arousal.

Maggie didn't need any urging. Her fingers curle
around the silken steel that proclaimed his masculin
ity. She was awed by the delicate pulse that bea
against her palm. He'd never let her hold him like this
saying it was too much, that his control wouldn't stan
it. She'd argue, but her protests would fade as h
brought her to the peak of arousal with his mouth, hi
hands . . . shooting her thoughts into a sensual obliv
ion where her only focus was what he wanted her t
feel.

He'd given and given without ever appearing to take
yet she'd always known she'd pleased him. She tol
him so.

"I'm not talking about sex," he said when he coul

catch a breath. His hips rocked slightly as she stroked him, lightly at first and then with more confidence. He gave himself another moment to luxuriate in the erotic play, then gently pulled her hand away. His own hands came up to rest on her shoulders, turning her to face the mirror as he moved behind her. "The proof that you arouse me isn't something I can hide. You can see it, you can touch it. But when I fell in love with you—"

"You knew then?" Her heart skipped a beat as she realized what he was saying. It wasn't just the baby—and the miscarriage—that made him want to be with her. "You knew you loved me?"

He nodded. "It's the pleasure I was talking about," he said, pushing aside the silk on her shoulder and taking tiny nips of the flesh there. "You filled me with something I couldn't identify, something I'd never felt with another woman. For a while I pretended it was just another level of sex."

She sighed, unable to stifle her self-satisfied smirk. "Kind of hard to think beyond that, isn't it?"

"Mmm." His tongue whipped across her shoulder, tasting her as her body heated under his touch. "But I was experienced enough to realize this was something I'd never felt before."

She snuggled back against his chest, her eyes closing as she enjoyed the delightful sensual forays of his mouth, his hard arousal nudging her back—a delicious reminder of the heights they'd soon scale.

He loved her . . . and she believed him. It made everything right.

"How did you know it was love?" she asked, letting her head fall back on his shoulder.

"I didn't. I just knew it was something I didn't dare let you see." His thumbs hooked under the straps of the blouse and slipped it from her shoulders, pulling at the material until the soft curves of her breasts were pushing for release. He stopped just when her nipples would be exposed, holding the fabric tautly as he sought her gaze. "A week after you left, I finally admitted it to myself."

"A week," she breathed, a sudden chill pulling her from the sensual whirlpool. "Then you would have never told me if I hadn't had to call—"

He laughed, a short, self-deprecating bark that told her there was more to this. "The same day I figured it out, I came running after you. I saw you outside your house with your brother and jumped to the conclusion that you were already enjoying the attentions of another man. I left."

She stared at his reflection as she adjusted to the implications of that. "But you never ever questioned that the baby was yours. If you thought I was seeing another man—"

His hand roughly cupped her chin, bringing her mouth to meet his in a kiss that was almost brutal in its intensity. When it was over, he told her the truth. "I never doubted," he said gruffly, his lips touching hers as he spoke. "Not even for a second."

Her thank you was lost in the surrender of her mouth to his as he claimed her for a kiss that punctuated his words. "I love you, Maggie Cooper," he said softly.

Her heart nearly turned over as she again heard the words that were like a dream come true. She smiled, then tried to turn so that she could kiss him properly.

"Uh uh." His fingers tightened around the material of her blouse, forcing her to stand as she was—facing the mirror with him gazing at her reflection. "Don't turn around yet, Maggie love. I want to watch your eyes."

"You could do that without a mirror," she said, then caught her breath as he dragged the straps down to her elbows—exposing her breasts, which were already swollen and aching for his touch.

"Not like this, love," he murmured, wrapping one arm around her waist to hold her to his chest and tracing the line between her breasts with the other. "This way, I get to watch you watch."

Her eyes widened as she followed the slow movement of his hands. She was captivated by the sight of his lightly stroking fingers, embarrassment a fleeting thing that was easily overcome by the excitement. It was incredibly erotic to see the smile on his face and know it was because he was enjoying her arousal. She couldn't help but cry out when his fingers skated up the curve of her breast to flick the already distended nipple. She sagged against him as he plucked at it with his fingers, and was vaguely wondering how long she could take the sensual torture when he left that breast and began to torment the other.

Then her gaze followed his as his hands crept downward. Slowly, deliberately, he gathered her skirt until it was bunched at her waist, revealing the exotic lingerie she'd bought amid a thousand blushes. She'd persevered because she'd hoped it would give him pleasure.

It did.

He touched the silken panties and growled his approval. "You're so beautiful," he murmured, nuzzling aside a wisp of hair so that he could touch her forehead with his lips. She watched spellbound as he toyed with the lacy garters, her mouth drying from her quick, excited breaths when he nimbly undid the tiny loops and catches and tossed the garment aside. Her nylons were the next to go, Will disappearing from the mirrored reflection to kneel at her feet as he rolled down the silky stockings. He pressed lightly on her instep when it was time to pull them off, rewarding her with a quick, hot kiss on her thigh before rising behind her again. Then he shoved her skirt over her hips and to the floor.

She watched, nearly crazy from the attention, as he molded one hand around a breast and slid the other across her tummy. Her heart thudded as his fingers edged over to her hip, where they slipped under the thin panties and tugged. "Take these off."

She gasped at the sensual directive, but didn't do as he asked because it went way beyond her nerve.

"Now, Maggie," he insisted in a low voice that played havoc with her senses. "Take them off now. And don't forget to watch."

She was convinced that she couldn't do it. But then she looked into his eyes and suddenly—*urgently*—understood the excitement. Slowly, she pulled her arms from the blouse, patting at the fabric as it settled around her waist. Her eyes never left his as she skirted his hand at her hip and touched the lace and satin that rested there.

She hesitated, and he smiled, a sensual, knowing smile that made her forget her inhibitions and want to rush to please him. She stilled that hurried impulse, though, and made herself do it slowly. Smoothing her palms on her thighs first, she watched his eyes darken as she carefully, painstakingly pulled the bit of material down her hips. She never saw what he saw then, so absorbed was she by the darkening in his gaze.

His hand slid across her belly and lower, completely covering what she had revealed as he murmured words of love and praise in a voice that was husky with passion. Maggie couldn't help it when her eyelids fluttered shut. She cried out in a kind of frustrated relief as he touched her there for what felt like the very first time.

It seemed like hours later—or was it only moments?— when he lifted her into his arms and carried her to the bed. She was senseless from the pleasure of his touch, enraged by the strength of his control, incoherent with the need to feel him inside her. She pleaded and cajoled, caressing him with a fervor that was returned in kind until the sheets were damp with their sweat and they had to push them aside. Time and time again she pressed him to finish it until she realized, finally, that he wouldn't surrender to her demands, not yet.

He wouldn't give her the release she so desperately wanted because he was waiting for something. It penetrated her cloudy thoughts, a persistent niggling that made her frantic in her efforts to please him. What could she give him that he didn't already have? she asked herself, drawing his tongue into her mouth as her fingers prodded the flesh of his back and buttocks, his arousal hard and demanding between them. *What was he waiting for?*

Suddenly she knew.

"I love you," she said. She felt him tremble as he lay upon her and knew she'd got it right.

"You've never said that before." There was wonder in his voice as he parted her legs with his knees. He hesitated at the damp entrance of her womb, then eased back to rest on his haunches, a slow smile curving his lips.

That she had him where she wanted him—more or less—was an understatement.

"You said I didn't have to say it," she reminded him, watching as he reached for the packet he'd tossed onto the table earlier. "You said you knew just by looking in my eyes that I was falling in love with you."

"I lied." His gaze drifted from her swollen lips to her mussed hair, then on to the arms she'd flung above her head. The faint sheen of sweat made her body glisten in the muted light from the dresser. She was voluptuous in her surrender, and he knew he'd never seen her looking more beautiful. "It seems I've been waiting to hear those words forever."

"I love you." She rather liked the sound of them herself, although she could have sworn her voice had lost at least an octave, because they came out sounding incredibly husky. She cleared her throat and croaked it again. "I love you. What's *wrong* with my voice?"

"Nothing a little water won't cure," he said. His own throat was dried out from the exertion of the last hour or so. "Remind me to get you some. Later."

He lowered himself onto his forearms, and a shudder traveled through his entire body as Maggie reached down to guide his entrance. Or was it her trembling that he felt? He didn't know.

Two seconds later, sheathed in her warmth, warmed by her love, he quit thinking altogether.

Eleven

Dawn found the lovers wrapped in each other's arms, tired yet not asleep. At eight Will called his office and canceled his trip to Reno. Then he tracked down Biff and asked if he could divert the movers and have Maggie's things stowed in a storeroom for a day.

Biff said that he thought he could manage.

Still, they didn't sleep. Maggie barely gave Will enough time to hang up the phone before she attacked him.

It was noon before they gave in to the need for rest, late afternoon when Will awakened Maggie with firm, careful strokes that were meant to excite rather than soothe.

That evening, he loaded her into his four by four for a drive.

Pausing just shy of the passenger door, Maggie stepped back a couple of steps and pointed to the lettering on the side of the truck.

"Eddie Bauer?" she asked, her eyebrows askew at the seeming incongruity. "I thought you said your name was Will."

"It's the Eddie Bauer model of the Explor—" Will

stopped before he got too deep into what was a useless explanation. Sometimes he forgot that Bambi Bubblehead was a deliberate act.

"An Explorer." Maggie smirked as she climbed into the luxurious leather seat. "Seems to me that a truck driver would have a field day with a vehicle like this."

"I'm not—"

"Why, I'll bet there's a fifth wheel around here somewhere," she said, and craned her neck to look into the rear compartment.

"It's under—"

"Hard to believe that you got so defensive about this," she went on, easing into a comfortable slouch. "I can't imagine there are too many truck drivers that fare as well."

"I'm not—"

She grinned and he gave up . . . just gave up and drove her to his redwood-and-glass home. Perched on the side of a hill just above Lake Tahoe, the multistoried structure was an architectural triumph in terms of function and design. Maggie got so excited when she saw it, she left Bambi in the truck and beat a path for the front door.

Both the classy, well-equipped kitchen and the comfortable but decidedly masculine living room met with her approval before she gravitated to the wall of windows that showcased the lake and surrounding mountains.

"Do you ever get used to it?" she asked, her voice filled with awe as her gaze flitted from the peaks to the water and back again.

"Not really," he said. He embraced her from behind. "But some days I appreciate it more than others."

She sighed. "I don't think I could ever wake up to that sight and not feel blessed. What a marvelous way to start your day—easing into that first cup of coffee as you check up on the view to see what's changed since you last looked."

"That can be arranged," he murmured, dipping his head to nibble at her ear. "Just say yes and I'll have you moved in here before the sun sets." The almost blinding ball of fire was already touching the jagged peaks, a fact that neither of them missed.

Maggie laughed and turned in his embrace, her hands finding their way around his neck. "Bribery will get you nowhere," she said, "but if you want us to sleep over here every once in a while instead of my apartment, I don't think I'd mind too much."

"Is tonight too soon for you?" His hands stroked her back in long, seductive sweeps. "I've wanted you in my own bed for so long, I'm not certain I can wait another night."

She brushed her lips across his chin and pretended to consider his request. "Mind if I check the weather report first? I'd hate for my first morning here to be cloudy."

He swatted her backside and told her that if she was going to be picky, she could make her own coffee. And then, for the very first time in his home, he kissed her on the lips and whispered promises of love that seized her heart and made her believe in tomorrow.

The next morning Maggie told him they could spend however many nights he wanted in his home, because the sheer pleasure of waking up to the magnificent view was infinitely superior to the piece of lake she could see from her apartment.

She wasn't moving in, though, she insisted. Just visiting a lot. There was a difference.

He chafed at the restrictions she'd put on living with him, but didn't argue, not then. Privately, he decided that if she didn't give up the hotel apartment by Christmas, he'd put on the pressure. He wanted her with him and *dammit,* this was his home and it was where she belonged.

He'd never been a patient man, however, and he knew the waiting would be hard.

In the meantime, he made her swear she wouldn't try to drive that little car of hers up the steep, winding road that led to his house after the snow started. She warned him that he was lapsing into an overprotective frame of mind that was better suited for the father of a teenager, but he wouldn't even discuss it. She'd either do as he asked or he'd put a net over that orange bug.

Even though she'd managed perfectly well last spring with chains and snow tires?

Even then.

She swore, and then she agreed, reluctantly admitting that while she might be an independent woman, she wasn't stupid.

Will agreed with both.

Later that morning, he took her back to the hotel and introduced her to her new boss, Angelo DiPietro. On leaving a few minutes later, he kissed her in front of DiPietro and everyone else in the banquet offices, leaving her flushed and furious and wondering why he'd felt it necessary to be so blatant about his possession.

After he'd left, Angelo just shrugged and said, "Italian men are like that. They want everyone to know when a woman is off-limits. It is in their nature to be possessive."

"As far as I know," Maggie said, trying to control the furious blush that colored her face, "Will doesn't have a single ounce of Italian blood in his body."

"Then you should be happy, Margaret," Angelo said, insisting on using her given name. "In this modern world that we live in, there aren't many men who are so open with their feelings. That he loves you is something everyone here now knows. How can that be a bad thing?"

How indeed? Maggie felt her heart lift at the unexpected encouragement, then had to drag her attention to the banquet preparations the older man was discussing. There wasn't, it seemed, time to give her a gradual introduction to the work she was expected to do.

Angelo tossed her into the melee headfirst and dove in behind her.

And so it began.

They found a place together that was better than

anything either had ever had before . . . and they knew it. The ease with which they slipped into a loving, sharing relationship went unquestioned. They didn't have to try to make it work. It just did.

Because Maggie loved Will, she was willing to do whatever it took to keep him. For the time being, that simply meant staying quiet regarding any hints of permanence. She knew that she couldn't stay silent forever, but then, she had to believe that Will would eventually come to realize that marriage wasn't the beginning of the end. She *had* to believe, because anything else was inconceivable. Unthinkable, really. She wanted him forever. She wanted children. The two were inextricably linked.

In the meantime, she lay with him at night and prayed that her hopes for a shared future were founded in truth.

She'd never been a patient woman, and the waiting was hard.

Perhaps to make up for what he couldn't give her, Will opened every other aspect of his life to Maggie. He shared business concerns and listened with respect to any suggestions she might offer, because he'd discovered that she had a knack for putting her finger on loose ends or untried solutions.

He made sure she got to know those people who were important to him, Casey and Harriet and Biff in particular. While Harriet pretty much kept to her own schedule outside of the hotel managing a pair of novelty shops that catered to the constant flow of tourists, Maggie soon came to rely on her for female companionship. Whenever the "guys" had a night out, doing whatever it was that guys did when they were together, Maggie and Harriet joined forces and did exactly as they pleased.

As for Biff, Maggie became so friendly with him, she soon talked him into giving her skiing lessons that winter. Will would have thought Biff knew better, especially after hearing tales of the Turquoise Terror. But he didn't interfere because, like it or not, Maggie was determined to ski, and he figured that as long as there was someone willing to teach her, he wouldn't have to.

"I value our relationship enough not to want to destroy it unnecessarily," he told her.

"Chicken," she scoffed. "Never mind. I'd rather learn from Biff any day than from the fourth runner up in last year's Old Geezers' Slalom Race."

"I came in third," he said, affronted that she'd forgotten.

"Whatever."

That afternoon she cornered Biff to ask him if he'd go with her to the ski rental shop when it opened next month, because she'd had some trouble there last year and needed support.

Biff agreed, with the condition that she leave the selection of equipment to the experts. Maggie pretended she hadn't heard and told him she was planning on buying the purple ski outfit she'd seen in the showcase of the hotel's clothing shop.

After hearing about that, Will considered warning Biff about Bambi, but decided against it. Biff, he decided, could handle just about anything that came his way.

Thus Will's friends became Maggie's. There was one person, however, that she never got around to meeting: Cheryl, the tall, black-haired beauty Will had wanted to avoid that first night he made love to Maggie.

Maggie had spotted her the first day she started work. And the second. And the third. Always from a distance, usually hanging on to a man. Maggie had been working there a week and was sitting in the lounge with Biff when Cheryl came in and joined another couple at a corner table.

"Does that woman have a job in this hotel that I haven't heard about?" she asked, her mouth curving down in a grimace.

"Not unless you call man hunting a job."

"That's why she's always here?" Maggie asked. "I can hardly go a day without seeing her somewhere in the building."

Biff shrugged. "I guess she got used to hanging

around here when she was dating Will. It's as good a place as any to meet people."

"You mean men," Maggie said, her frown deepening. "Do you think she's still after Will?" Not that she'd catch him, of course. Maggie knew better than to worry about that. It was just that it irked her to see Cheryl every time she looked up. Way up. The woman was easily ten inches taller than Maggie.

"Why don't you ask Will?" Biff suggested, and got to his feet.

"Ask Will what?" Will asked from behind her. Leaning down, he dropped a kiss on the side of her neck, then threw himself into a chair with his back to the corner in question.

Maggie flushed. "Nothing important," she said weakly, watching as Biff sauntered away without so much as a "see you later."

Obviously Biff wasn't nearly as curious about Cheryl as Maggie was. She lifted her glass of soda to her lips and winced as raucous laughter rang out from the corner table.

Will's glance shot over to the table before returning to Maggie, the light of understanding in his eyes. "Is Cheryl giving you a hard time?" he asked quietly.

She shook her head and hunched down in the chair. "How can she give me a hard time when I haven't even met her?"

A single eyebrow raised. "You *want* to meet her?"

"That's not what I mean," she said wearily. "It's just that she's almost part of the furniture around here."

"What piece of furniture does she remind you of?"

"How about a tallboy dresser?" she said disparagingly, wishing Bambi had a better answer.

"And that makes you unhappy?"

She sighed. "It's just that I remember that you had a relationship and I can't help but think she wants you back and—"

"And you think I'll be tempted?" he asked softly, leaning forward to tip her face up with his fingers.

Maggie looked into eyes that were filled with nothing

but love, love for her, and she knew she'd been foolish even to mention it.

"Cheryl and I were through before I ever met you," he said.

"You loved her?"

He shook his head slowly. "I enjoyed her. And I like to think that she enjoyed being with me. But I never made her any promises, just as she didn't make any to me. If she's having trouble understanding that it's over, there's nothing more I can do except give her the space and time to get used to it."

Maggie had to admire the way he didn't have anything bad to say about the woman who had been his lover. It was over and done with, she realized. If she had to trip over Cheryl every now and again, she shouldn't get worked up about it. Although it was a bit difficult to trip over a tallboy. Too bad she couldn't be an ottoman.

"Maybe I won't have to scratch her eyes out after all," she said meekly as she worked out the mathematics of squeezing those incredibly long limbs into something that people would put their feet on.

Bambi thought it was a terrific idea.

"You're not tall enough for that to be much of a threat," Will teased, totally missing the wicked gleam in her eyes as he rose from his chair and reached out a hand to help her up.

"If she were a building, she'd be a skyscraper," Maggie muttered, then added under her breath, "Just in case, I think I'll start wearing high heels to work. Never know when they'll come in handy."

"Did you say something was dandy?" he asked, guiding her out of the lounge and away from the laughter that was too bright, too brittle.

Maggie looked up at him and smiled broadly. "I was just wondering if Cheryl knew about Bambi."

He shot her a worried glance. "What about Bambi?"

She shrugged. "Nothing much. It's just that Bambi never did care for skyscrapers."

"Skyscrapers?"

"Umm." She caught Will's hand and tugged in the

general direction of the elevator. "They're so much more vulnerable to natural disasters than single-story buildings, don't you think?"

"Natural disasters?" he asked, then decided he didn't want to know. Not that he'd even understand, of course. He never really caught up when Maggie reverted to her ditzier alter ego. Taking the lead with a determination born of desperation, he pulled her into the elevator and punched the button for her floor, then covered her mouth with his own in an attempt to forestall her answer.

Bambi Bubblehead popped up just often enough to keep Will on his toes.

The warm summer that had lingered into the last weeks of September not so much faded gradually as it abruptly disappeared. One afternoon people were enjoying the lakeside amusements in shorts and T-shirts, and the next morning they were wondering where they'd stored their woollies.

Over the next few days frost touched the aspen, setting off a glorious explosion of color that was a visual treat amidst the warning that winter would be early and fierce.

Maggie recorded it all in her journal, a computer record now because everything seemed so urgent and typing was far quicker than writing it out longhand. As meaningful as the journal was to her, though, she almost always found herself rushing through it so as to have time to work on the stories that were figments of her imagination and bursting with lives of their own.

She was constantly frustrated that she had so little time to spend on them.

One night as Will was waiting for her to dress for dinner, he seated himself in front of her computer and asked her what she used it for. Games, she half fibbed, then stopped breathing as he switched on the screen and began to scan the menu.

"What do you keep under the file that's labeled 'Mine'?" he asked.

"Nothing important." That was a complete lie, and she froze for a second as she searched frantically for a diversion. "If you're looking for the games, they're in the folder marked 'Games.'"

"Tricky place to hide them," he said, then accessed the file. Soon he was shooting down spaceships without ever noticing the odd shade of white she'd turned.

Nothing important, she repeated silently. Just her life. And her secrets.

It bothered her that she didn't trust Will enough to share her secrets with him. But they weren't really secrets, she argued. Her journal was a diary that couldn't possibly be of interest to anyone but herself—unless he wanted to read the bits about himself and sorry, that was off-limits.

Her stories, on the other hand, were another thing altogether. She didn't think she'd mind so much if he read those.

Not that she'd ever get up the nerve to show him, of course. She'd rather be stuck in the middle of Skiers' Hell than face the embarrassment of having Will try to find something nice to say about her work.

Later that night, when he was sound asleep and the hotel lay quiet in the threshold of dawn, Maggie copied a few special computer files onto a pair of floppy disks and hid them beneath her long underwear.

Then she fell into an exhausted sleep beside the man who had almost exposed her dreams.

As the October nights nudged persistently at the daylight hours, Maggie threw herself into her work with a fervor that was typical of how she tackled everything. It was an interesting job with a diverse range of functions that varied hourly. She learned menus, room capacities, seating layouts, schedules, and coordination from the highly experienced catering manager. The headwaiter taught her how to set a table for an eight-course meal, who to call if a waiter didn't show for work, and how to persuade guests to deposit used cocktail toothpicks somewhere besides on the floor. The chef drilled into her the essentials of providing him with menus and head counts as soon as she knew them, why a dinner for fifty could only stretch so far if she estimated too low, and what to do with the leftovers if she came in high.

The variety of information blended with knowledge she brought from other jobs, and she found herself catching on quickly. All of the training was on the job, some of it taking place on the run between crises or even midevent. Maggie learned to anticipate if she could and cope if she hadn't.

She was doing well enough in three weeks to be trusted to make minor decisions—such as how many water glasses were needed on a conference table and which of the busboys could be trusted to post the week's schedule on the bulletin board for her.

Angelo was out of the office when Biff dropped by to test her newfound expertise.

"Your party of bridesmaids is getting out of hand," he said, pushing some papers aside so he could perch on the corner of her desk.

"They're models, not bridesmaids," she said without looking up. There was a stack of papers nose high on her desk and she was determined to get through it. "And they're modeling bridal gowns. Don't you know anything?"

"All I know is they're getting roaring drunk in my lounge."

"What are they doing in there?" she asked, still not paying him much attention. "They're supposed to be down in the main ballroom."

"I'm not their nanny," he pointed out. "And until that person shows up, do you think I should call in the riot squad or just hose them down every now and again?"

Maggie looked up from her work, horrified. "Don't even think it!" she commanded. "I saw those dresses and they've got to be worth a fortune! Can you imagine the bill they'd hit us with if we—" Then she saw mischief in his laughing eyes and knew she'd been had.

Without a word she slipped a hand into the bottom drawer and brought out a long gun. It was the pump action type, accurate to thirty feet.

At five, she blew him away. Water spat out of the orange barrel, plastering him in one shot.

"What the—" Biff was off her desk and on the floor before she could pump in a second round. He was a rolling target, but Maggie was merciless. She tracked him from behind the desk with the weapon, soaking the back of his shirt before she remembered that he might not have another handy.

"I surrender! I surrender!" he shouted.

Puckering her lips, she blew "smoke" from the tip of the gun and holstered it in her belt. Biff slowly got up and was a tad wary as he approached her desk.

"The next time you decide to waltz in here and give me heart failure," she drawled, "remember that I've got protection. Pass the word, bartender."

Biff grinned and tugged at his wet shirt, his gaze going across the room to where a huddle of waiters were gawking at them. "I think the word's going to get around fast enough, partner," he said, resuming his perch as she settled back into her chair. "Where the hell did you get that thing anyway?"

"One of the waiters confiscated it from a guest last night," she said, smiling up at Biff and wondering where he'd learned to move so quickly. He'd been on the floor practically before she'd got off her first shot. "I suppose I'll have to give it back if he asks for it."

"If someone doesn't confiscate it from you first," he warned, plucking at his shirt again as the water cooled on his skin.

"Was there something in particular you wanted?" Her hand rested on the gun, reminding Biff that she wasn't interested in any more false alarms. "Or did you just come up here to make me crazy?"

He grinned. "Actually, I thought I'd see how you were getting along."

"I'm getting along just fine—or I was until you showed up. And I'm finding it hard to believe you can't handle a couple of models. Having confidence problems, Biff?"

"Now that I know they're only playacting, I might show a little more interest," he murmured. "There was a redhead that was absolutely stunning."

Maggie pulled a newly laundered waiter's shirt from the locker behind her and handed it to him. "Put this on before you catch pneumonia."

"I will if you tell me how things are going with you," he said, unbuttoning his shirt and shrugging out of it.

"Fine." She fingered the trigger of the water gun. "As you can see, I've got things under control here."

The laughter left his eyes. "That's not what I'm talking about, Maggie. What I really want to know is if that smile you have on your face all the time is real—or if you're still hurting."

"Hurting?"

She didn't like the way this was going. He rested his knuckles on her desk and leaned down so that their words wouldn't go any further. "I'm your friend, Maggie. I know I'm being clumsy as hell about this, but I wanted you to know that I'm around if you want to talk about the baby."

Her eyes rounded with confusion. "How did you know?" she whispered.

"About the baby?"

She nodded.

"I flew Will to Vacaville that night when he couldn't find his pilot."

"And he told you." She hadn't realized . . . hadn't imagined that Will would tell anyone. It surprised her to realize she didn't mind, not since it was Biff.

She trusted Biff.

"He was hurting, Maggie," Biff said. "I think he still is."

"Me too." She smiled weakly, tears brimming but not falling. "Not as much as before. We talk about it every once in a while, Will and I. Now we do, that is." She added sheepishly, "Before, in the beginning, all I wanted to do was put it behind me so I wouldn't feel so incredibly sad all the time."

"And now?"

She swallowed and tried to smile. "And now, well, now I'm so much better. I usually manage to get through the day without crying all over my desk."

"That's probably a good sign," he said, smiling at her encouragingly as he pushed his arms through the sleeves of the dry shirt.

"I worry about forgetting, though," she said meditatively. "I don't think I want to forget, not entirely."

He started buttoning the shirt. "You won't. But you'll accept it and put it behind you."

She sighed and nodded.

"But if you ever need—"

"An ear to bend?" she asked softly, lifting her gaze to his.

He nodded. "Something like that. You can usually find me if you look hard enough."

"Why on earth would she want to bother?" Will asked. He was leaning inside the door, his hands hooked on the door frame so that he was only halfway inside. "Seems to me we get enough of you around here as it is."

Maggie's smile, which had been wistful just a moment before, suddenly brightened. She pushed back her chair and ran to the door, curling into a place under his arm as though she'd had years of practice doing just that. "He was just threatening to take me to lunch if you didn't show up in time," she said, laughing when Will said something succinct and to the point about what Biff could do with lunch.

"After," Will added, "you tell me what you're doing half naked in front of my—" He hesitated, suddenly aware he didn't feel comfortable using any of the titles available. Girlfriend was sophomoric, but calling her his lover was tawdry.

Maggie was the woman he loved, but he didn't know what to call her.

"In front of your . . . what?" Biff asked with distinct interest.

"My Maggie, of course," Will improvised. "If I were a jealous man, I'd call you out."

"You'd have to stand in line. Your *Maggie*," he said with mocking emphasis on the name, "has already taken her shots at me today." He finished tucking the shirt into his trousers and grabbed the wet one off the floor. "Now if the two of you will excuse me, there's a certain redhead sitting in the lounge that I need to meet."

He twisted the wet shirt between his hands, and added in an aside to Will, "If you're going to have lunch with Dead Eye here, I'd advise you to make sure she checks her weapon at the door. There won't be enough dry shirts in all of Dodge City once she starts blasting away with that thing."

Will's gaze sharpened on the orange plastic toy dangling from Maggie's belt, and he took Biff's advice without a second thought. Biff was no sooner out the door when Will confiscated the weapon in question. On their way to lunch, he turned it over to a responsible adult.

Casey's eyes gleamed mischievously as he turned the orange gun over in his hands.

Later that night, as Maggie slept in his arms and the stars edged their way across the sky, Will thought about Biff and the things Maggie had told him Biff had said to her. It was as if he'd gone through this kind of pain himself, Maggie had said, because he truly understood.

Biff was a sensitive, caring friend, she added just moments before falling asleep.

Will stared out the window into the night sky and wondered what Maggie would say if she'd seen the negligent ease with which Biff had dispatched those two hoodlums last year. Then he smiled, remembering Biff's soaked shirt.

Maggie was too much of a contradiction herself to worry about other peoples' little inconsistencies.

• • •

At the end of six weeks as Angelo's assistant, Maggie admitted to herself that catering was not her dream career. The disappointment of yet another dead end in the career department weighed heavily on her, but she tried to keep it in perspective.

There were lots of things she hadn't tried yet. Professional dancing, for one. And sports broadcasting. She wondered if there were any openings for gaffers on *The Arsenio Hall Show.* Then she wondered exactly what a gaffer was—or did.

She was pleased to note she'd retained a sense of humor in her disappointment.

Walking quickly down the carpeted steps that led to the banquet room, she checked to ensure the luncheon there was proceeding according to schedule, then crossed to the rest room to check her appearance. She was meeting Will for lunch, a fact that filled her with the same anticipation it did every time he managed to get away from his office.

Being with Will was as exciting today as it had been on their first meeting. Maggie grinned at her reflection and flipped on the tap to wash her hands. She heard the door close, a faint whoosh above the noise of running water, and Maggie looked up to find she was no longer alone.

"I wondered if I'd ever get a chance to talk to you," the newcomer said, "when Will or one of his cronies wasn't around."

Maggie's smile disappeared as she recognized the black-haired beauty in the mirror. Cheryl. As many times as she'd seen her around the hotel, they'd never spoken.

She found it hard to get up the enthusiasm for it now.

"I don't think we've met," Maggie said, plucking a towel from the dispenser. She dried her hands quickly, then held out her right one as she said, "I'm Maggie Cooper."

When Cheryl only stared at her hand, Maggie

dropped it to her side, berating herself for imagining this would be a civilized encounter.

"I know who you are," Cheryl said, her gaze hardening. "You're the flavor of the month."

"Excuse me?" *Flavor of the month?* Maggie glanced at the door and prayed one of the ladies across the hall would take time out from her appetizer to save her.

"I'm talking about Will, of course," Cheryl went on, drifting closer until there were just inches between them.

Maggie held her ground. Not that she had much choice, what with the sink at her back and Cheryl between her and the door. It irked her that she had to tilt her head way back just to maintain eye contact, but she held on to her temper.

"Will Jackson?" she asked mildly—as if there were another!

"Mmm. He changes women as regularly as most men change their ties."

Maggie gritted her teeth, determined the other woman wouldn't get a rise out of her. "Will changes women?" She laughed with as much humor as she could muster. "We're obviously talking about two different men! The Will I know is much more fastidious than that. Besides, I know for a fact that he prefers to be taller than the woman he dances with." She threw that in because she was getting a crick in her neck.

Cheryl's mouth tightened in disgruntled fury and she lashed out with what she thought was her heavy gun. "How long has it been for you now? One month? Two?" When Maggie didn't answer, she smiled tightly and added, "It won't last much longer, you know. It never does with him."

Maggie believed in Will, though, a much stronger influence than the ridiculous warnings from a woman scorned. She was also getting weary of the cat game Cheryl seemed determined to play. "Give it up, Cheryl," she said harshly. "There's nothing you can say that will in any way affect my relationship with Will."

Without waiting to see how her words would impact

on the other woman, Maggie stepped around her and walked to the door. She was nearly there when Cheryl said, "Not even if I tell you that he's seeing another woman?"

Maggie shook her head and almost laughed. "Get real, Cheryl. If he was seeing another woman, why on earth would you be wasting your time in trying to torment me?"

Cheryl's mouth was gaping open unattractively as Maggie turned away and pushed through the door. She caught it just before it could swing closed behind her and added, "Don't ever forget that skyscrapers are vulnerable to disaster." Then she let the door close and took a deep cleansing breath. It was over now, the confrontation she'd half dreaded ever since she'd returned to Tahoe. Cheryl was part of Will's past and Maggie could accept that. Cheryl also had nothing to do with his future. Maggie knew that with a certainty that was unshakable. But if Cheryl wanted a fight, she'd get one.

Maggie was smiling as she skipped up the stairs to the restaurant where she was to meet Will for lunch. She'd been confident enough to face Cheryl without doubting. She'd trusted Will's love for her enough not to fall prey to Cheryl's malicious lies.

Confidence, she thought, was something she very much enjoyed having—and that was all she had on her mind when she stepped into Will's arms and kissed him hello.

It was the second week in November before Maggie got up enough nerve to tell Angelo she was quitting.

She was a little piqued when she realized she hadn't taken him by surprise. "I thought you said I was doing a good job," she said. "How can you be so calm about me quitting?"

He shrugged. "Doing a good job and being satisfied in your work are two separate things. Me, I feel good about my work. It's what I like doing. I'd probably do it even if it didn't pay so good."

She blinked. "Catering pays good?" That was news to her.

"At a certain level," he said, his eyes twinkling from beneath bushy brows. "But I get the feeling that money isn't going to change your mind."

Maggie sighed and twiddled her thumbs.

Angelo swiveled in his chair, then swung back holding the platter of in-house pastries that he kept on his credenza for clients and out-of-sorts assistants. Thrusting a fork across his desk, he waited until she was deep into a flaky napoleon before continuing.

"Have you told Will yet?"

She shook her head. "I thought I'd wait until you found someone to replace me. Maybe by that time I'll have something else lined up."

"You have to realize that he'll know as soon as I tell Casey that I'm looking," Angelo said, a reproving half smile crinkling on his face. "Do you really want it to come from anyone but you?"

"I suppose not," she said meekly.

He gave her a minute to think about it, then asked her what kind of job she had in mind.

"Professional dancer. Sports broadcaster. Gaffer." She shrugged and finished off the rich pastry. "I haven't tried any of those yet."

She suffered Angelo's disbelief in silence as she licked her fork clean. She wasn't worried about telling Will. He would just help her to redirect and that would be that. Another job, another stab at finding herself.

Maybe her luck would improve with age. She'd tell him tonight, she decided.

Angelo cleared his throat and she looked up, startled to realize he was waiting for something. "Yes, Angelo?"

"Margaret, it seems to me that you're trying very hard to be something that you're not."

"I was kidding about the professional dancer part," she said, surprised that he would take her teasing so seriously. "I didn't mean it. I'll find a normal job that's just right up my alley."

He shook his head. "I don't think you're kidding."

She grinned and leaned across the desk to pat his hand. "Trust me, Angelo. I couldn't do the tango if I tried."

"This isn't about dancing at all," he said slowly but with a sureness that defied any hesitation. "It's about dreams."

She stared at him, wondering how it was that a man she knew so little could see so much of her soul. There was a catch in her voice when she was finally able to say, "Not a dream, Angelo. A fantasy."

"A fantasy," he said, his voice a hushed whisper in the suddenly quiet office. "Is that what you call your dream?"

She nodded, unable to speak about something she'd never discussed with another human being.

"What is your fantasy, Margaret?" he asked. "What is it that you want to do that you're afraid to try?"

Maggie was saved from answering by the ringing of the phone. She grabbed it, a lifeline that was too little too late. Her secrets were secrets no more. She could tell that just by looking at Angelo's smile of smug determination.

As the desk clerk asked her if it was possible to cater a dinner for twenty-five for that night, she pounced on the challenge with a professional zealousness that would have impressed any catering manager in the world, with the exception of the one sitting across the desk from her.

Him she ignored.

Fantasies and dreams took a poor second to the necessity of doing a real job that paid real money in the real world.

Twelve

"I quit my job today."

Will glanced up from the wine menu he was studying and said, "That was quick." He snapped the leather folder shut and ordered champagne.

Of all the reactions she'd expected, this wasn't one of them. Pushing the sleeves of her soft wool sweater up to her elbows, she folded her arms on the table and considered the man seated opposite her.

It irked her that he could be so casual about it.

Will stared back at her, smiling as he appreciated the lovely picture she made in the soft candlelight. The sweater was new, a frosty shade of gray that reminded him of the color of her eyes when they were clouded with desire.

He'd told her as much when she'd tried the sweater on at the shop. His consciously provocative words had brought a rush of color to her face as she'd scanned the vicinity for anyone who might have overheard.

The sweater was just one of many new things she'd purchased this past month during a marathon shopping expedition that she'd insisted was necessary to supplement her meager cold-weather wardrobe. He had gone along with her, not because he liked to shop but because he wanted to make sure she bought enough to last the winter.

The quantity of new clothes was a subtle affirmation of her determination to stay. He had been relieved without revealing it.

Just as he didn't reveal his total panic at the news that she'd quit her job. That she wouldn't be able to find one in Tahoe that she enjoyed carried with it consequences he was unwilling to face.

"Champagne?" Maggie asked when he appeared to be waiting for her to say something. "Now, I realize that you've never been real happy with the long hours I've sometimes had to work, but don't you think this is going a little overboard?"

"The champagne is because you've finally admitted that you were in the wrong job. Whether or not I'm happy about it is immaterial."

Her brows knit in a puzzled frown. "How come you're not surprised?"

"Maggie love, we've been practically living in each other's pockets for the last two months. How could I *not* know that you weren't happy with the job?"

She thought about that for a moment. "It's not that I wasn't happy exactly," she said slowly. "It's just that it's not what I want to be doing this time next year. I decided to get out before Angelo wasted any more time on me."

He nodded as if he actually understood. "There's nothing wrong with that decision, Maggie. The only person that's upset about it is you."

He didn't know the half of it, Maggie thought. She swallowed over the lump in her throat and sat back as the waiter ceremoniously presented the bottle for Will's inspection.

They were eating dinner out that night. Not out as in at one of the hotel dining rooms, but out out. The restaurant was part of an inn that was located just a few blocks downhill from the hotel. It was, according to the brochure, an "exquisitely comfortable establishment with a reputation for elegantly unique bedrooms set above a dining room of superior standards."

Maggie had read the blurb and told Will it meant the rooms were fun, the food was terrific, and you got to pay a premium for both. Laughing over it as they waited in the cosy bar for a table, Maggie had wondered if whatever writing skills she had might be channeled into the advertising field.

It occurred to her then that she was grasping at straws.

The muted pop of the champagne being uncorked blended with the subdued sounds from the surrounding tables. Maggie took an appraising look around the room. Its accents of pink and mauve subtly enhanced the sense of warmth and easy comfort that she'd felt the moment they'd first entered. The elegance of crystal and silver blended with exposed brick and rough-hewn beams in a surprisingly pleasing style. Waiters in dinner jackets drifted among the tables without hovering, attending to the needs of the more casually dressed patrons with an expertise that was neither intimidating nor condescending.

She liked this place very much.

"I've wanted to bring you here for a long time," Will said, deliberately breaking into her thoughts. That she had quit her job was obviously worrying her, and he didn't want that.

He wanted her to smile.

She did. "Then why didn't you?"

"Because it's a special place, and I wanted to save it for a special occasion."

Her heart tripped into double time and she shuttered her gaze, letting it drift downward so that he couldn't see the excitement his words had prompted. *A special place. A special occasion.* Did it mean what she wanted it to mean? Had Will finally realized that marriage was the only way they could build a real future together?

Had a mere two months awakened him to the rewards of commitment?

She decided to play it cool, a difficult proposition

considering the wildly fluctuating rhythm of her pulse. What occasion?" she asked. She looked to see him holding his tulip-shaped flute of champagne. She lifted her own with a hand that trembled visibly.

"What occasion, she asks!" he teased, then relented as he noticed how tense she'd become. "Well, I don't know about you, but I personally think that the completion of the two happiest months in my life is worth a celebration." He tipped his glass to meet hers. "Happy anniversary, Maggie. I love you."

She heard the faint tinkle of crystal touching, realized that she was lifting her glass to her lips, even tasted the sparkling wine, but only in an abstract way, as if it were happening to another woman and not to her.

Happy anniversary. The words burned like an illicit brand upon her heart. A toast in celebration of the *relationship* between them.

A relationship, not a marriage. Would he ever want anything more from her than she'd already given? Would he ever want the commitment that was so much more than a few words by a judge and the piece of paper that made it all legal?

She blinked a couple of times to erase from her expression any trace of her sudden disquiet, smiled carefully, took another sip from her glass, and said, "Happy anniversary to you too. I never would have pegged you for the sentimental type."

A waiter swooped down with menus and a litany of things that weren't on it, satisfactorily keeping Will from noticing that she wasn't as cheerful as the occasion might warrant. She tuned out the intricately detailed verbal report and hid behind the tall menu when the waiter was done.

She couldn't lose hope. Wouldn't. Happy anniversary. A relationship with milestones. It wasn't enough, she raged in silence. And then, quite suddenly, she remembered what else Will had said. *The two happiest months in my life . . . I love you.*

Only a nitwit would be unhappy to hear words like

that! she chided herself. She smiled brilliantly and knew that her mood swing had been noted, because he looked a little confused.

Served him right, she thought. She took a long drink of the fizzy wine as she contemplated the future and how long it would take to convince Will that she intended to be an intrinsic part of his happiness for a long time to come. Forever, to put a point on it.

She smiled as her heart recovered from the unexpected freefall. It was going to turn out okay. She just had to believe. Knowing full well there was challenge in the gaze she linked with his, she swallowed the rest of her champagne and held out her glass for more.

On Will's signal, the waiter opened a second bottle of champagne. Maggie dipped a finger of deep-fried mozzarella cheese into the hot mustard sauce and watched as her glass was again filled with the delicious wine.

That she was feeling luxuriously bubbly was a natural consequence of all the champagne. Maggie didn't care. She was, in fact, feeling quite reckless with the unaccustomed alcohol. She teased Will with a verve she'd never before dared, whispering enticing tidbits when she thought no one would hear, rubbing her bare foot on his leg when she could find it.

With every glass, she lost another level of discretion.

Will recognized the symptoms and was satisfied. He buttered a slice of sourdough bread and put it on the plate in front of Maggie, assuming she'd eat anything as long as she didn't have to work too hard at it.

He was right. She ate the bread without any urging on his part. Soon, he knew—as long as he was careful not to refill her glass—the bread would begin to counter the effects of the alcohol.

In the meantime, he had a few questions to ask her. There was something about her job that she wasn't telling him. He'd known for weeks that she wasn't being completely open, but he hadn't wanted to corner her on it.

Give her time, he'd told himself. She'll let you know when she's ready. But that was before she quit her job with Angelo after only two months.

It was time that she let him in on the big picture. He loved her too much to go on not knowing it all.

"Maggie?" he said softly.

"Hmm?" She swallowed more champagne and grinned at him.

"I'm sorry the job didn't work out for you." He gave her another piece of bread, then added, "Have you got any ideas about what you want to do next?"

Elbow on the table, she rested her chin on her fist and sighed. "You know, Will, some days I get the feeling that I'm never going to find the right job."

The waiter paused to top off her glass before disappearing again. Maggie took another sip, then continued. "I mean, it's not like I don't try." Her tone became plaintive as she gave full vent to her feelings. "But every time I get a new job, it's the same story. I learn how to do it—and I usually get pretty good at most things—but once I get a certain level, I just seem to get bored."

"Maybe you're not looking in the right places."

"Easy for you to say," she scoffed, her chin teetering off its perch before she stabilized. "Your dream was rational."

"Dream?" His gaze narrowed on her face as he realized he was getting close.

"That's what I said, Will." She wagged her finger at him. "Your dream was rational. Dipso facto, you succeeded."

Dipso facto? Wasn't that supposed to be *ipso facto?* He grinned at the slip à la Bambi, even as he wondered if it was intentional. With all the champagne he'd practically poured down her throat, it was easy to believe Maggie had merely goofed.

"What dream are you talking about?" he asked, and had to wait for her to take another sip of champagne before she answered.

"Angelo understands dreams," she said unexpectedly. "That's probably why he didn't mind when I quit."

Angelo? She'd talked to Angelo about this? Will grew more persistent. "What dreams, Maggie?"

"You know what I mean, Will." Her gaze wandered over his shoulder until it was no longer focused. "The thing you want to be when you grow up. Like a princess. Or a rock star."

He chuckled. "I never wanted to be a princess. I swear it."

"Of course not," she said patiently, not appreciating the joke. "You were more practical than some of us. I bet you always knew what you wanted to be."

"And what was my dream then?"

"Your dream must have been business. Real estate and all those other things you do now are satisfying a dream."

"How can you tell?"

"Because you're happy about it." She refocused on his face, her expression just a little impatient as she tried to find the words that would make him understand. "It excites you in a way that maybe doing a different job wouldn't."

"I never thought about it that way," he said. "I just always did what I wanted."

"That's because you've got self-confidence clear down to your toenails," she muttered. "Not all of us are that blessed."

He muffled a laugh when her mouth twitched her disapproval. Maggie was definitely cranky with him, although he was beginning to realize it wasn't so much his fault as it was disgust at her own lack of confidence.

And here he'd thought they'd taken care of that once upon a time. Perhaps they had, he mused, but only in one direction.

He honed in on dreams because it seemed to be the key to her distress. "Tell me about your dreams," he said softly, motioning away the waiter and their dinner. He was afraid the interruption would sabotage his efforts. They could eat anytime, but he might never get another opportunity for Maggie to open up to him. "What do you want to be that's so fantastic?"

"Promise me you won't laugh?" she said hesitantly, her eyes sending a silent plea of understanding.

He nodded and clenched his teeth. He knew whatever she said was going to be so outrageous, he was bound to have a serious problem with control.

He wouldn't laugh. Not even if she said she wanted to be a truck driver.

"I want to be a writer?"

He blinked. "A writer? What's so impossible about that?"

She smiled condescendingly. "You don't understand, Will. I want to be a writer." When he didn't say anything, she added, "I want to write books. Short stories. Things that people read because they want to."

"And?" He couldn't see the problem. Maggie was a talented, competent woman. If she wanted to write, then all she had to do was sit down and do it. There was always the chance that she wouldn't be as good as she wanted to be, but life was full of risks.

The Maggie he loved wouldn't be afraid of risk.

She shook her head. "And nothing. You wanted to know my dream. There it is." She took a large gulp of water and looked worriedly around the room. "I wonder where dinner got to?"

"Don't worry about dinner," he said impatiently. "Go back to the part about wanting to be a writer. What is there about it that makes it such an impossible dream? Is there a reason that I don't know about? Were you told in college that you have no talent? Did you take a writing class and flunk out?"

She shook her head slowly, a tiny smile reaching her eyes.

"Then why don't you give it a try?" he asked, thoroughly puzzled.

"Not all of us have your confidence, Will. Did it ever occur to you that I might be afraid?"

He stared across the table at the woman with whom he'd shared more of his life than any other single person and shook his head. "No, Maggie, it never crossed my mind. Not even once."

In that moment, Maggie Cooper realized that the only thing stopping her from living her dream was herself. In that moment, she stopped being afraid.

"What if I can't produce anything that anyone wants to read?" she asked, chewing aggressively on the steak that was not so much overdone as it was, well, settled. Somehow, it tasted as though it had been cooked and rewarmed. She was surprised, what with the reputation of the inn being what it was and all.

"If it's what you really want to do with your life," Will said, "then I guess you'll just have to keep trying. Have you done any writing at all or is everything in your head?"

She grinned. "In my head, mostly. But I've kept a journal almost from the time I learned how to push a pencil. And I've got some stories I started a while back. It's all on the computer under 'Mine.'"

"No it's not," he said, wiping the napkin across his mouth. "That file disappeared weeks ago."

"You noticed?"

"I noticed. Where'd you put it?"

"Under my long underwear."

He laughed loud and long in the nearly vacant room, then asked her if she'd put it back where it belonged so he could read it.

"I've never let anyone read anything before," she said, hesitating at what felt like the edge of a cliff.

Will put down his fork and said, "I'm not anyone. I'm the man who loves you."

"You really want to read it?" she asked quietly, then added, "Not my journal, but the other stuff?" She couldn't let him read the journal, not yet.

"Yes, love," he said, his voice equally as hushed. "I'll read it because it's a part of you that I don't know yet."

"And then you'll tell me if it's any good?"

He shook his head. "No, Maggie, my love. What I have to say should have nothing to do with it. I'm reading it for me, not for you."

"But how will I know?" Her fingers drummed nervously on the white linen cloth as she stared at him in frustration. The waiter took their plates, served coffee, and faded away as she pondered the problem.

"It's *your* dream, Maggie," Will finally said, reaching across the table to still her hand with his. "You have to believe in yourself first or you'll never get anywhere with it."

"I believe in me," she said shortly. "It's just that I'd like a second opinion."

"You'd trust me for that?" he asked, amused that she'd managed to get exactly what she wanted.

She leaned across the table, beckoning him with her index finger to draw close. With the candle flame casting light on their faces and her eyes warming to a frankly sensual glow, she said, "I had less trouble getting feedback out of you when I wanted you to make love with me that first time. Now, are we going to do this the easy way or do I have to sic Bambi on you?"

He watched spellbound as she drew the tip of her tongue across her bottom lip, leaving it glistening in the flickering light of the candle. Her gaze heated to smoldering, and he knew that their lovemaking that night would be akin to playing with fire.

He wanted the fire.

Suddenly, he pushed back from the table and reached around to pull her out of her chair. "If Bambi doesn't know any better than to tease me in public, she'd better be aware that there are consequences," he said as he hustled her from the dining room.

The consequences were handled neatly and to the point. Will checked them into the inn for the night and with an impatience that left her breathless, taught her an erotic lesson in teasing that she'd not soon forget.

They returned to the hotel early the next morning. Maggie dug the floppy disk out from under her long johns, showed Will how to operate the printer, then went into the bathroom to shower.

She'd just finished drying her hair and was pulling on

her sweater to the accompaniment of the muted hum of the laser printer, when Will dropped the bomb.

"We can set up an office for you in the loft," he said, "unless you think you'll be distracted by the view. I don't know how you like to work."

"The loft?" she asked, pulling on the matching wool skirt and smoothing the sweater over her hips. "Why should I want to work over at your place when all my stuff is already here?"

He swiveled in the chair to face her, his expression unreadable. "I assumed you understood," he said evenly. "You lost the apartment with the job. I can't justify letting you stay here if you're not working at the hotel." It was a crock, of course, but he couldn't think of a better lever.

He wanted her with him and he was tired of waiting.

That this might be a consequence of quitting her job had never crossed Maggie's mind. She took a deep breath and presented an option. "I could always find another apartment."

"Not an easy thing to do now that the snow is falling."

"Not easy, perhaps. But certainly not impossible."

The printer hummed to a stop. He turned, punched a couple of keys, and it went on with the next segment. Then he rose from the desk and came to her.

Still in her stocking feet, she felt even shorter than usual as he towered over her, but there was nothing for it. She wouldn't retreat and couldn't imagine that he would sit down and talk this over at eye level.

He was going to use every advantage he had, and she knew it.

"I want you to move in with me, Maggie," he said firmly. "We spend most of our nights there anyway. This running back and forth is nonsense."

"I told you before that I wouldn't feel right about living with you if we weren't married." She held her ground, knowing that if she gave in on this last thing, she might never get through to him.

Will expelled a frustrated breath and wrapped his fingers around her arms, acting for all the world like he was going to squeeze some sense into her. "But you don't *want* to get married."

"Who says I don't?" she asked in a voice that was almost a whisper. She hadn't expected it to come like this, the one argument that would tear them apart if he wasn't willing to back down. She'd thought he would be more patient, that it would be months before he began to insist.

"You said . . ." he began, but she held up her hand to cut him off.

"No, Will. *You* said you didn't want to marry." She swallowed and watched as his expression raced from frustration to disbelief and finally to a stunned realization. She waited, and as his eyes darkened in anger, the gray becoming cold and forbidding, she knew that he understood.

"*You* said you didn't want to marry," she repeated. "*I* didn't say anything at all."

The only noise in the room was the hum of the printer as it pumped out page after page of a dream that would be meaningless if Will walked away. She knew that his hands felt the shudder of fear that shot through her, but she didn't care.

He had to know that she was risking their love for something important.

"I don't believe in marriage," he said evenly, his expression daring her to convince him otherwise.

She didn't even try. It wasn't something she could do for him. "I know."

His hands dropped from her arms, but he continued to hold her with his gaze for a long moment before saying, "Then I guess we'll just have to find you an apartment, won't we?"

Thirteen

Maggie knew that morning that she'd lost. It took her four days to decide what to do about it.

In the quiet of the early afternoon lull that followed lunch, she sat behind her desk and stared out the window at the dark storm clouds and the swiftly falling snow. There were two notes on the desk. The one for Biff explained why she wouldn't be able to meet him for her first ski lesson the next morning.

Her note to Will was shorter. It said merely that she needed some time alone.

She didn't know what else to say.

That was why she was leaving. She needed to make a decision about what she was going to do and she couldn't do that with Will behaving for all the world like nothing had changed between them.

On the surface, their relationship was as it was before. They laughed, kissed, and made love with the same tenderness and passion. Maggie continued working in the catering offices, having agreed to stay until Angelo could hunt up a replacement. Will dropped in to take her to lunch with the same frequency as he had before they'd argued.

Together they searched the classifieds for a suitable apartment.

If she caught him looking at her in a way that was faintly bewildered, she put it down to her own tension, because the next moment the expression would be gone and he'd be talking about the weather or something equally as trivial.

She didn't understand him anymore.

Four days, and he hadn't said a word about her writing. He'd taken her stories with him that morning and hadn't mentioned them since.

Her insecurities blossomed with every passing day. Were they as bad as all that? she wondered, fearing that her worst-case scenario had come true and he couldn't find a single good thing to say about them.

Perhaps he didn't have time to read them.

Perhaps he didn't want to.

She had to get a grip on herself. That was why she was going away.

Standing, she cleared her desk with a precision that belied her shattering nerves and picked up the notes. In her room, she took just ten minutes to change and pack for the two days that she'd be gone. She wouldn't need much, not in Vacaville. She'd decided to go back to check on her house and have a talk with the realtor who was managing it for her. There were friends she'd kept in contact with that she would like to see. Basically, she wanted to touch base with the life she used to have.

She needed to know if it was what she wanted to go back to.

She dropped off her key and the notes as she passed the front desk, grateful that Casey wasn't around. He'd see the overnight bag slung over her shoulder and ask questions that she wasn't in the mood to answer.

Neither was she in the mood for Cheryl, but that didn't seem to sway the Fates. The black-haired woman was standing in the direct path between her and the front door. Maggie could see her orange Volkswagen parked outside, tires chained and ready to tackle the deepening snow. She could have gone around and out another door, but with every minute that ticked away, the storm worsened.

She had to get across the pass at Echo Summit before it closed.

She zipped up her parka and headed for the door.

"Going someplace?"

She should have known she wouldn't get away scot-free. She stopped and said hello as pleasantly as she could, because if she couldn't tell Will why she was leaving, she certainly wasn't going to stand around discussing it with one of his former lovers. She quickly added good-bye and turned to leave.

"I heard you were looking for an apartment," Cheryl said from behind her. "I told you it wouldn't last."

Enough was enough. Maggie let the overnight bag slip from her shoulder and fall to the floor, turning as it did to face the woman who didn't know when to quit. "Cheryl," she said softly, "if you don't keep your nose out of my business, I'm going to have to do something that you won't like."

The other woman just laughed and measured her with a disdainful glance. "What's a shrimp like you going to do that I would even notice?"

The last straw. Maggie glared at the woman as she counted to ten. She even tried to reason with herself, but it didn't change anything. Cheryl was standing there smirking down at her with that idiot smile on her face, and Maggie knew she had to wipe it off. With a sigh that came out sounding like "You asked for it," she crossed to the reception desk, circled around it to Casey's office, and went inside. She shouldn't do it, she told herself. She was better than this, certainly more mature.

She did it anyway.

Accurate to thirty feet, and Casey had left it loaded. Maggie stepped out from behind the reception desk and took aim. Pump, fire, bull's-eye. Twice more she worked the firing mechanism, then she tossed the empty water gun to a grinning bell captain, who didn't seem to find anything amiss with her marksmanship. Keeping in mind that Cheryl's sense of humor was almost certainly dampened by the large wet spot on her silk dress, Maggie skirted the woman with caution. She snagged her bag and was walking out the door when a strange shrieking noise assaulted her ears.

She walked faster. Raising her hand toward the parking attendant, she caught the keys he tossed her and went to her car. It was cold and not particularly interested in starting again, but she paid it no heed. She was leaving and this was her transportation, like it or not.

When the car grumbled into life, Maggie set her mind to the long drive ahead, barely paying attention to the swirling snow that slowed her progress. It wasn't until she was halfway down the hill toward the main drag that she realized the storm had turned into a full-fledged blizzard.

They would have told her at the desk if the pass was closed, she reasoned. Or they would have, if she'd told them where she was going. She weighed the pros and cons of pressing on versus turning around and waiting for the storm to pass.

It couldn't possibly be as bad as it looked. After all, she could still see at least a block. Checking to be sure there was no one behind her, she hit her brakes and was satisfied when the chains grabbed the road's surface.

The car was a champ. With a stomach-clenching sense of adventure, Maggie slipped her foot off the brake and proceeded sedately down the hill.

She was going to make a run for it.

"I want her to hear it from you," Will said into the phone. "She seems to need a second opinion and we might as well make it one that counts."

He listened to the voice at the other end for a few moments. He made satisfied noises and added, "I'll tell her you're going to be calling, then. And make sure you're firm with her. Don't let her fool you into thinking she doesn't have anything to send. I've read the stories and they're terrific."

There was a smile of supreme satisfaction on his face when he replaced the receiver. For four days he'd been trying to get hold of Michael, a friend who also happened to be a big-shot editor in New York City. Michael had been at a writers' conference or something, a nuisance as far as Will was concerned, because he hadn't dared breathe a word about his intentions to Maggie—not until Michael had actually agreed.

He hadn't wanted to get her hopes up needlessly. Of course, now she had to go through the process of submitting and waiting and hoping . . . a torturous procedure that normally took months for beginning authors. Michael had promised to expedite things on his end.

With luck, Maggie would only have to hold her breath for a week or so. And he'd do his damnedest to distract her.

He was so impressed by her talent, it never occurred to him that she wouldn't succeed. Now all he had to do was hold her hand until someone that counted could give her the reassurance she needed.

Maybe now she'd quit treating him like he was going to walk out on her just because she'd dared to tell him she wanted to get married. It had angered him at first—until he realized she was doing no more than matching his honesty.

Reverting to the status quo was the best solution all around. For now. He hadn't lost a single bit of his determination to change her mind, but he'd learned a degree of patience since she'd hit him with that bit about marriage.

It would take time, but she would come around. He knew she would.

Checking his watch, he realized it was time to pick her up. They'd made plans to eat at his home that night, and her car was restricted to the parking lot for the duration of the storm.

Shoving his arms into his thick sheepskin coat, he

said good night to his secretary, pulled the collar snug around his neck, and walked hatless into the swirling snow. Although it was only four o'clock, the dark of night had already fallen upon the mountains. He was grateful he didn't have to worry about Maggie being out in the gathering storm.

He lost that comforting feeling the moment he arrived at the hotel and found her missing.

"How long has she been gone?"

"The bell captain said the shootout was right around two o'clock," Casey said.

"Why the hell didn't you call me then?" he demanded, his angry gaze spearing Casey. "That was three hours ago, for God's sake!" He looked down to see Biff's restraining hand on his arm.

"Take it easy, Will," Biff said. "This isn't anyone's fault."

Will was about to shake him off when he glanced up to see the calm reproof in Biff's expression. He was right, of course. This wasn't Casey's fault.

It was his own. If he'd just disabled that stupid car instead of going with her to get the chains put on it, she wouldn't have been able to go anywhere.

Where in the hell was she?

"Sorry," he said shortly. "I'm not thinking straight."

Casey nodded. "I only just found out myself. No one thought anything about it until Biff picked up his note from her. He'd just called me when you arrived."

Will took a deep breath and tried not to panic. His own note had been brief and to the point. *I need some time alone.*

So where had she run to?

They were in Casey's office, the three of them pulling on cold-weather gear—boots, gloves, wool scarves—as they prepared to go out and search for Maggie. They'd each take a truck, naturally, but there was no telling how many times they'd have to get out and walk, perhaps flagging down passing cars to see if she'd passed that way.

The hotel operators were in the process of calling every hotel, restaurant, and hospital in the vicinity, checking obvious places where she might have gone. So far they'd had no luck, and the highway patrol hadn't been able to do any more than say they'd put her on the list and promise to report in if they spotted her. With manpower levels already stretched past the limit, it was the best they could do.

Casey had ordered cellular phones put into the trucks, along with hot drinks, blankets, and food. There was no telling how long they'd be out there. According to the weather report, the storm wouldn't peak until the early hours of morning.

They didn't have a clue which way she'd gone, so they were shooting out in three directions. There wasn't any use hoping she'd gotten over the pass or through on any other road. The last road out had closed at three, long before she could have made it that far. But hundreds of cars were still caught between the snow gates and town. With communication in the zero-visibility storm restricted to word of mouth, it would take hours to get everyone turned around.

She could run out of gas.

She could run into a ditch.

She could abandon the car and walk just ten feet in the wrong direction—ten feet into a blizzard that didn't forgive such human errors.

Will swallowed hard and prayed that she stayed with the car.

They were ready. Will studied the two men who were going out to find Maggie. There was a measure of assurance in their eyes that told him everything he needed to know.

If she was out there, they'd find her.

He nodded once, then led the way out of the office and the hotel. They each double-checked the survival gear and the cellular phones before disappearing into the white night.

It was a quarter past five. She'd been out there for three hours.

For the thirty-second wretched time that miserable day, Maggie stopped the car, got out, and prayed that no one would crash into her as she tugged the clumps of ice from the windshield wipers.

This was not her idea of fun.

When the biggest clumps were gone, she traipsed around to the other side and did it again. It wouldn't last five minutes, she knew.

But for five minutes she would be able to see well enough to keep going, and that's what it was all about.

She was going back to Will and was determined to get there tonight. Preferably unfrozen. Climbing back into the car, she slipped the gear into first and tackled the hill.

Going back to Will was a great deal more difficult than leaving him.

It was, in fact, a lot of hard work. It had begun with that traffic jam on the road up the mountain. Cars passing, cars getting stuck, cars going fearlessly into the great white eclipse ahead and then disappearing.

It had been a nightmare of the very worst kind—the kind you can't wake up from. Maggie had made a plan and stuck with it from the moment she'd realized she wasn't going to get anywhere. Survival instincts had kicked into high gear once she'd quit feeling sorry for herself and realized that she was running away from the only man she would ever love.

Her plan was simple. It was called follow the leader.

She'd tucked her car behind a pickup that appeared to be going the right direction and stuck to it like glue—right up to the moment the driver guessed wrong and ended up in a ditch. Her chains had saved her from following by a hair's breath.

The pickup's driver had been as grateful for the ride back to town as she'd been for the extra pair of eyes in the whiteout. His name was Bill and she thought he might be around thirty or so, but that was only a guess. It was hard to attach an age to a nose sticking out of a parka hood. They had become friends in the way that only survivors could.

They talked about important things because this was scary stuff and neither wanted to go through it with a stranger. He told her about the girlfriend he'd been heading out to see, and was worried because he'd promised to take her to dinner and now he'd be lucky to get his truck out of the ditch before Thanksgiving.

He didn't know if his girlfriend would understand, but in the next second he realized that if she didn't, she wouldn't be any great loss. The circumstances were beyond his control and he wanted a woman who could understand that.

Maggie agreed, then invited Bill to share Thanksgiving dinner with her and Will. Or just with her if things didn't work out. Either way, Thanksgiving was for family and Bill was now a member.

Then she told him she was going back to Tahoe to move in with the man she loved. Marriage was just a piece of paper, after all, and if she had to live without it, she would.

She couldn't live without Will.

It didn't matter what he thought about her writing. Funny how her words came out sounding like Will's.

And so she and Bill talked, the white cocoon easing confessions and truths.

They crawled along the fifteen miles to civilization more slowly than it would have taken to walk, watching the gas gauge edge downward and trying not to worry because there were lots more people behind them who would pick them up if things went wrong.

If they could see them.

If they didn't run them over in the whiteout.

If they were really there. It was hard to know, visibility being the same behind as it was in front.

They stopped at the sixth gas station they came to, because it was the first one they'd seen that was open despite it only being seven o'clock. The little Volkswagen gamely lept the walls of drifted snow and slid into line behind at least eight other vehicles. The fact that the station was doing a booming business took nothing away from the humanitarian gesture of staying open in a blizzard. Maggie made a promise to herself that she'd write the owner a letter of gratitude as soon as she had a pencil and paper.

As soon as her fingers started working again, she amended. They'd sacrificed heat in the car in order to divert full power to the defroster, a decision that enabled them to actually see as far as the wipers. That was necessary because they had to know the second the ice started clumping on the rubber blades.

She dropped Bill off at a bar a block from his home, insisting she could do the rest alone and not really giving him any choice in the matter. She had just turned off the main drag to tackle the hill leading up to the hotel when the lights went out.

Not the Volkswagen, but the town. Street lights, signals, homes, everything went black.

For the thirty-third wretched time that miserable day, Maggie stopped the car, got out, and prayed that no one would smash into her as she tugged the clumps of ice from the wipers. Then she cleaned the snow off the headlights because if it was the only light she was going to have, she'd best make the most of it.

This was not her idea of fun.

Biff found the Volkswagen half-buried in a snowdrift.

Maggie wasn't in it, but the engine was still slightly warm, so he knew she had to be close.

He got on the phone and called Will, giving him the exact location as well as the direction of her footprints. He passed on the same information to Casey.

Putting the truck into low gear, he turned the headlamps on bright and began tracking. Casey and Will caught up with him about ten minutes later. They hadn't been far away, what with the search narrowing to the hillside and knowing from Bill that she'd been heading to the hotel.

Bill had been an unexpected piece of luck.

One of the hotel operators had got the idea to call bars after she finished with her second round of restaurants. What with one thing leading to another, she'd found herself talking to a man named Bill.

The three trucks pressed slowly but steadily through the swirling blizzard, following tracks that were quickly fading in the storm. She hadn't sought shelter in a nearby house, and that stumped them all. It appeared as though she had a destination.

Suddenly, Will knew where she was headed. Her tracks faded into nothing just fifty feet short of the inn where he'd got her tipsy on champagne. He brought his truck even with Biff's, then passed him and led the way.

It was the only place she could be.

He prayed she was there.

She was huddled in front of the fire, wrapped nose to toe in a blanket and drinking from a cup that an extremely kind woman named Carissa had to hold for her because her fingers weren't working yet. It was an embarrassing position to be in, but Maggie was too cold to be embarrassed.

She took a cautious sip of the warmed spirits and was just about to ask Carissa if she wouldn't mind unzipping her pants for her so she could use the restroom, when three burly shapes crowded into the lounge.

Biff, Casey, and Will pulled the hoods back on their parkas and stared at her.

Biff looked relieved.

Casey looked like he wanted a little of whatever she was drinking.

Will, on the other hand, managed to mask whatever he was thinking.

She found that hard to cope with and turned away.

"Kind of a cold evening to be going out for dinner,"

he said. Then she asked if the three of them would like
o join her for a meal. Reservations weren't necessary.

If you wanted to eat by candlelight, she added,
because the power was still out.

If you didn't mind stew. Anything else needed power,
but the stew was already made.

If you were hungry. She was famished. Not a new
condition, she admitted, but certainly not something to
be ignored.

Then she asked if anyone had any money because
she'd forgot to bring her purse when she left the car.
She knew she was babbling, but it was so obvious that
they'd been out in the blizzard looking for her and *she'd
never meant to cause anyone worry!*

Carissa handed Biff the mug and left the four of them
alone in the bar.

"Bambi returns," Biff said, shaking his head as he
moved closer to her. "If you ever pull another stunt like
that, Dead Eye, I'll personally see to it that you never
see snow again." He held the cup to her lips.

"It wasn't a stunt," she said after she took a sip. "I'm
sorry if I caused you any trouble."

"No trouble," he said gently. "Worry, yes, but no
trouble." He dropped a kiss on her forehead and walked
away, handing the cup to Casey as he left the bar.

"The next time you decide to stage a shoot-out in the
lobby," Casey said, "give me some warning."

"Why?"

He grinned. "Because I want to be there. Word is that
you soaked Cheryl with your first shot. Three was
overkill."

"I had the advantage of surprise."

He hugged her quickly and in a whisper told her the
gun was back in his office. If she ever needed it.

He left the room, setting the mug on the bar when
Will wouldn't take it.

They were alone.

Will shrugged off his tawny sheepskin parka, tossing
it over a nearby chair as he walked toward her. She

watched uneasily, and knew she had a lot to apologize for.

She'd caused him to worry, and that was inexcusable. Even though leaving was something she'd done for herself, she'd never once thought how it might affect him. Even if she hadn't been caught in the storm, she should have known he would worry. Just because he wouldn't marry her didn't mean she could ever deny the fact that he loved her.

"I was coming back," she said as he neared. "It doesn't matter if you don't want to get married. I'll move into your house tomorrow."

He didn't say anything, just stared at her with eyes that were so gray, all the blue had nearly vanished. She was frightened then, afraid that the mere thought of leaving had dealt a blow to their relationship he was unwilling to overlook.

"I'll do anything you say," she said in a very soft voice, feeling his breath on her face. "I'll live with you and have your children and be whatever you want me to be."

"Children?" he repeated, his hands on her shoulders now, warming her in a way that far surpassed the flames at her back. "You want children?"

"How could you not know that?" she asked, giving herself up to the heated massage of his hands. "When I lost our child, it nearly destroyed me. It all became so real—children, family, sharing our lives."

"And in order to have children, we have to marry."

She lifted her gaze to his and shook her head. "Only if that's the way you want it to be," she said, her heart nearly falling into pieces as she sought a compromise that would save their love. "Before . . . The reason I left . . . I couldn't imagine one without the other. But out there in the storm, I realized I was being selfish."

She wasn't the only one, Will thought. Nearly losing her because of his own selfishly stubborn beliefs had humbled him. "What if I said I wouldn't give you any children unless you married me?" he asked, his heart thumping against his ribs as he suddenly understood.

Marriage was for life . . . and he couldn't imagine spending his life without Maggie. The institution that had always seemed to mock love was suddenly a commitment he refused to live without. Only through loving Maggie did he understand the necessity for that commitment.

Her breath caught in her throat as she realized they'd both won. She swallowed over the sudden inclination to cry, because this moment wasn't one to cry over.

It was a moment to rejoice.

"Will you marry me, Maggie?" he asked, pulling her up to stand, blanket and all, dragging her into his warmth, his life.

"Is tomorrow too soon?" she asked quietly. "I don't think I can stand waiting that long . . . to begin."

He said yes. And then, when it was agreed, he pressed his lips to hers and tasted the promise of tomorrow.

Later, when he broke their kiss to tell her about Michael wanting to see her work, she couldn't stand still from the excitement of it all. She laughed and giggled and jumped up and down. She plagued him for details in between kissing him with an enthusiasm he found wildly infectious.

To put it mildly, he thought she was pleased with the news.

Margaret Ann Cooper—*Mac to my friends but you can call me Maggie*—had never been so happy in her entire life.

Epilogue

When Biff showed up at her door the next afternoon with a bridal gown draped across his arms, she didn't ask where he'd found it.

There were depths to Biff one didn't question.

It was a glorious silk gown of ice pink with a closely fitted bodice and full skirt and train. She loved it.

Harriet helped her to dress, pulling her hair back and catching it up with a confection of lace and white flowers that she'd found in the florist's shop in the lobby. She lent Maggie her long off-white gloves that she'd worn at her own wedding, and held Maggie's hand when she started to tremble at the speed with which things were happening.

It wasn't that she was nervous about what she was about to do. Quite the opposite. She had never been so certain of anything in her life.

She trembled because she was living her dream . . . and her dream was Will. She had other dreams, to be sure. Without this one, though, they hardly counted.

She loved him with an intensity that made anything else that she'd ever wanted fade into insignificance.

It was time.

Taking the bouquet of hothouse tulips from Harriet, she left her apartment and walked with firm steps to meet her destiny.

The music began as she arrived in the foyer to the grand ballroom.

Angelo met her there and took her hand. When he placed it on his arm, she looked up at the smiling Italian and was glad he wanted to do this for her. If Matt had been there, it would have fallen to him to give away his sister in marriage. But the snow and their haste prohibited all but the necessities . . . a man and a woman, standing before God and His witnesses, pledging their love for each other for as long as they both shall live.

She could see Will now, darkly handsome in formal clothes, standing beside Casey, Biff, and a man who must be the justice of the peace. They were at the end of an aisle that was graced with pine boughs and stretched the entire length of the ballroom. Even at that distance, she could feel the strength of his gaze. Falling into step beside Angelo, she locked her gaze with Will's and went forward to join with the man she loved.

Slowly, steadily, they passed the rows of chairs that were filled with hotel guests, waiters, and maids, until she was finally at the end. Angelo handed her off to Will with a kiss, and she gazed with complete happiness at the face of the man with whom she would spend the rest of her life.

They shared a smile of sweet promise, then turned eagerly to say their vows of love.

Their life together was about to begin . . . and they were ready to get on with it.

THE EDITOR'S CORNER

If there were a theme for next month's LOVESWEPTs, it might be "Pennies from Heaven," because in all six books something unexpected and wonderful seems to drop from above right into the lives of our heroes and heroines.

First, in **MELTDOWN**, LOVESWEPT #558, by new author Ruth Owen, a project that could mean a promotion at work falls into Chris Sheffield's lap. He'll work with Melanie Rollins on fine-tuning her superintelligent computer, Einstein, and together they'll reap the rewards. It's supposed to be strictly business between the handsome rogue and the brainy inventor, but then white-hot desire strikes like lightning. Don't miss this heartwarming story—and the humorous jive-talking, TV-shopping computer—from one of our New Faces of '92.

Troubles and thrills crash in on the heroine's vacation in Linda Cajio's **THE RELUCTANT PRINCE**, LOVESWEPT #559. A coup breaks out in the tiny country Emily Cooper is visiting, then she's kidnapped by a prince! Alex Kiros, who looks like any woman's dream of Prince Charming, has to get out of the country, and the only way is with Emily posing as his wife—a masquerade that has passionate results. Treat yourself to this wildly exciting, very touching romance from Linda.

Lynne Marie Bryant returns to LOVESWEPT with **SINGULAR ATTRACTION**, #560. And it's definitely singular how dashing fly-boy Devlin King swoops down from the skies, barely missing Kristi Bjornson's plane as he lands on an Alaskan lake. Worse, Kristi learns that Dev's family owns King Oil, the company she opposes in her work to save tundra swans. Rest assured, though, that Dev finds a way to mend their differences and claim her heart. This is pure romance set amid the wilderness beauty of the North. Welcome back, Lynne!

In **THE LAST WHITE KNIGHT** by Tami Hoag, LOVE-SWEPT #561, controversy descends on Horizon House, a halfway home for troubled girls. And like a golden-haired Sir Galahad, Senator Erik Gunther charges to the rescue, defending counselor Lynn Shaw's cause with compassion. Erik is the soul mate she's been looking for, but wouldn't a woman with her past tarnish his shining armor? Sexy and sensitive, **THE LAST WHITE KNIGHT** is one more superb love story from Tami.

The title of Glenna McReynolds's new LOVESWEPT, **A PIECE OF HEAVEN,** #562, gives you a clue as to how it fits into our theme. Tired of the rodeo circuit, Travis Cayou returns to the family ranch and thinks a piece of heaven must have fallen to earth when he sees the gorgeous new manager. Callie Michaels is exactly the kind of woman the six-feet-plus cowboy wants, but she's as skittish as a filly. Still, Travis knows just how to woo his shy love. . . . Glenna never fails to delight, and this vibrantly told story shows why.

Last, but never the least, is Doris Parmett with **FIERY ANGEL,** LOVESWEPT #563. When parachutist Roxy Harris tumbles out of the sky and into Dennis Jorden's arms, he knows that Fate has sent the lady just for him. But Roxy insists she has no time to tangle with temptation. Getting her to trade a lifetime of caution for reckless abandon in Dennis's arms means being persistent . . . and charming her socks off. **FIERY ANGEL** showcases Doris's delicious sense of humor and magic touch with the heart.

On sale this month from FANFARE are three fabulous novels and one exciting collection of short stories. Once again, *New York Times* bestselling author Amanda Quick returns to Regency England with **RAVISHED.** Sweeping from a cozy seaside village to the glittering ballrooms of fashionable London, this enthralling tale of a thoroughly mismatched couple poised to discover the rapture of love is Amanda Quick at her finest.

Three beloved romance authors combine their talents in **SOUTHERN NIGHTS,** an anthology of three original novellas that present the many faces of unexpected love. Here are *Summer Lightning* by Sandra Chastain, *Summer Heat* by Helen Mittermeyer, and *Summer Stranger* by Patricia Potter—stories that will make you shiver with the timeless passion of **SOUTHERN NIGHTS.**

In **THE PRINCESS** by Celia Brayfield, there is talk of what will be the wedding of the twentieth century. The groom is His Royal Highness, Prince Richard, wayward son of the House of Windsor. But who will be his bride? From Buckingham Palace to chilly Balmoral, **THE PRINCESS** is a fascinating look into the inner workings of British nobility.

The bestselling author of three highly praised novels, Ann Hood has fashioned an absorbing contemporary tale with **SOMETHING BLUE.** Rich in humor and wisdom, it tells the unforgettable story of three women navigating through the perils of romance, work, and friendship.

Also from Helen Mittermeyer is **THE PRINCESS OF THE VEIL,** on sale this month in the Doubleday hardcover edition. With this breathtakingly romantic tale of a Viking princess and a notorious Scottish chief, Helen makes an outstanding debut in historical romance.

Happy reading!

With warmest wishes,

Nita Taublib
Associate Publisher
LOVESWEPT and FANFARE

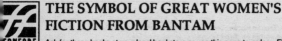

FANFARE

FANFARE

Rosanne Bittner

_____ 28599-8 EMBERS OF THE HEART . $4.50/5.50 in Canada

_____ 29033-9 IN THE SHADOW OF THE MOUNTAINS
$5.50/6.99 in Canada

_____ 28319-7 MONTANA WOMAN .... $4.50/5.50 in Canada

_____ 29014-2 SONG OF THE WOLF .... $4.99/5.99 in Canada

Deborah Smith

_____ 28759-1 THE BELOVED WOMAN .. $4.50/ 5.50 in Canada

_____ 29092-4 FOLLOW THE SUN .... $4.99/ 5.99 in Canada

_____ 29107-6 MIRACLE .... $4.50/ 5.50 in Canada

Tami Hoag

_____ 29053-3 MAGIC .... $3.99/4.99 in Canada

Dianne Edouard and Sandra Ware

_____ 28929-2 MORTAL SINS .... $4.99/5.99 in Canada

Kay Hooper

_____ 29256-0 THE MATCHMAKER, ... $4.50/5.50 in Canada

_____ 28953-5 STAR-CROSSED LOVERS .. $4.50/5.50 in Canada

Virginia Lynn

_____ 29257-9 CUTTER'S WOMAN, ... $4.50/4.50 in Canada

_____ 28622-6 RIVER'S DREAM, ... $3.95/4.95 in Canada

Patricia Potter

_____ 29071-1 LAWLESS .... $4.99/ 5.99 in Canada

_____ 29069-X RAINBOW .... $4.99/ 5.99 in Canada

Ask for these titles at your bookstore or use this page to order.

Please send me the books I have checked above. I am enclosing $ _____ (please add
$2.50 to cover postage and handling). Send check or money order, no cash or C. O. D.'s
please.

Mr./ Ms. _____

Address _____

City/ State/ Zip _____

Send order to: Bantam Books, Dept. FN, 414 East Golf Road, Des Plaines, IL 60016
Please allow four to six weeks for delivery.

Prices and availablity subject to change without notice.   FN 17 - 4/92